SINNERS, SAINTS,
AND
SCRATCH TICKETS

SINNERS, SAINTS,

AND

SCRATCH TICKETS

A Novel

GINA D'AGOSTA

ISBN: 978-0-9985-8170-5 (sc)
ISBN: 978-0-9985-8171-2 (e)

publisher name GMDbooks
Publisher address 511 West Wing St. Arlington Heights, IL 60005
Publisher phone # 6304538463
Legal Name Gina D'Agosta

Lulu Publishing Services rev. date: 04/04/2017

For my Mom

Here everybody has a neighbor, everybody has a friend, everybody has a reason to begin again.

—Bruce Springsteen, "Long Walk Home"

One Cherry

CHAPTER 1

Once upon a time,
there was a family
that was doing just fine.
But their story
isn't this story
in any of its tiny-town—
glory
be
to the father
who left them to rot,
hang on to what they've got
left
instead
of right
past the shining stars
at midnight,
the moon's blouse
undone.
Because every wrong turn
still leads to
something
or someone.

Alison yawned, sat up, and stretched her long, thin arms over her head. She smiled at a picture on a cluttered desk. It displayed the face of a large pale man with a soft yellow smile surrounded by coarse brown and gray facial hair and crow's-feet pulling his eyes toward dark curls that fanned outward under a faded baseball cap. "Good morning, Dad. You thinking of coming home today?" she asked the man in the picture. She kicked one bony knee over the side of the bed at a time, her eyes still fixed on her father's image.

At twenty-four, Alison's figure was that of a stretched-out child—no chest, no fat, no flaws, just smooth and straight. She was a tall, tan stick figure. She looked a little like her dad, except for the color of her skin, dark olive, and her smile, giant and thick like a banana. As she stood, her eyes found a calendar taped to her wall that featured a puffy white cat who had been wearing a flowered swimsuit for the entire month of June. It was by far the most thought-out feline clothing choice for the entire cast of cats in 1994 thus far. But Alison always looked forward to turning the month to see what the next feline was wearing. "Five years is a long ..." Her voice trailed off as she glanced back at her dad's face. "Don't worry; I haven't given up," she said, shaking her head back and forth.

She shuffled through the rubble on top of her desk and grabbed her cigarettes and lighter and a pile of papers, envelopes, stamps, and a pen. She carried them out of her bedroom toward the kitchen where her mom, Jean, and dog, Bob, were already sitting in chairs across the table from each other.

There was a romance brewing between the thick aroma of Folgers coffee grains and his mistress, the rain, who air-mailed her sloppy wet kisses through the screen of a window that had accidentally been left open. The coffeepot crackled. The thunder answered. Bob looked at the coffeepot, then the window, then Jean. Alison leaned against the door frame.

"Here, you can have sports," Jean said as she slid part of Monday's edition of the *Omaha World Herald* across the kitchen table to her dog, who put his head up on the table on top of the paper.

Although Jean didn't live in Omaha or anywhere close, she did live in Nebraska, in a town so small most people never even said its name, Trenton. They usually just referred to the group of houses and businesses there as Jasper County. Alison figured her mom felt cosmopolitan reading that big paper every morning. And on more than a few occasions, she had heard her mom tell strangers she lived in Omaha when asked where she was from. But her mom also hadn't seen her husband in five years and still wore her wedding ring, so Alison guessed there was a life that was her mother's and a whole other life that her mother pretended was hers.

"It's okay. It's just thunder," Jean explained to Bob, not looking up from a story about a football player who had the police chase him across California in a white Bronco after his ex-wife was murdered. Jean took a drag from a cigarette that should have been ashed four paragraphs ago.

"Sure sounds like he killed her," Jean commented.

Alison continued to stand in the doorway, waiting for her mother to notice her. She knew her mother was talking to Bob and not her. Jean looked at Bob as she spoke to him and paused before looking back down at the newspaper, as if he were able, just unwilling, to respond. He tilted his head one way. She tilted her head the other way. Bob barked.

"You're up early, Curly," Jean said excitedly when she noticed her youngest daughter leaning on the door frame with an armful of supplies. Alison's hair had never been curly, not even when she was little. It was long, straight, and the color of sand. But Jean had the habit of rhyming, at times, to lighten the mood—kind of like the way people say, "No way, José," Jean would say, "That's true, Lou," or, in this case, "You're up early, Curly."

"Why's it so fucking hot in here?" Alison asked, walking into the kitchen and throwing her materials down on the table. She sat down in front of them.

"Don't cuss, Gus."

"Well, it's fucking hot though," Alison said. Then she stood up, took off her Pink Panther pajama pants, threw them across the room, and sat back down. Bob jumped down from the chair he had been sitting in and raced across the kitchen to pick up Alison's pants and bring them back to her. When he dropped them in front of her, she bent over, picked them up, and threw them again.

Jean gave Alison a look. She took a sip of coffee, set it down, and said, "We do not sit at the kitchen table in our underwear."

"Maybe you don't. But I do."

When Bob raced back this time, he dropped the pants in front of Jean's feet. Jean sighed. "And we don't play fetch with each other's pants," she told Bob.

Alison rolled her giant green eyes.

"I already went through this page," Jean said, sliding a section of the paper that had all the addresses in it circled. Jean knew Alison's system, the way that her daughter scanned the newspaper for addresses each morning—a grocery store referred to in a closeout, a church mentioned in a remodel, a residence in an estate sale. Alison copied all of them onto envelopes, stuck a paper with her father's picture on it inside the envelope, sealed it, stamped it, and mailed it. Every once in a while, Alison included a little personal note with something like "Please help me find my father. Keep a flyer for yourself and pass one on to a friend or mail it to someplace far away." It depended on her mood, the time she had, the weather, and many other things. This was a system Alison had come up with that made her feel less sadness about her dad being gone. And no matter how many flaws there were to this system—because her father was most likely no longer in the state of Nebraska or anywhere close, if he was even alive—no matter how little success she had with it or how much crap her older sister, Sarah, gave her about it, she was doing *something* to find him.

"Thanks," Alison said, picking up one piece of paper from her pile, folding it, and putting it in an envelope. Across the top of the paper were the words "Missing: David Eugene Robbins, 6'9", 280 lbs, dark-brown and gray hair, brown eyes, facial hair." On the bottom, it read, "Please contact Alison Robbins at 1-302-779-2861 with any information." In the middle of the paper was the same picture of Alison's father that she kept in her bedroom. It was the way she remembered him—soft, kind, and weathered.

Alison was focused on folding papers and putting them in envelopes when her mother's concerned voice put a bullet hole in her concentration.

"I hope you haven't been wearing those since last Wednesday."

Alison looked up, annoyed and confused.

"Your underwear," Jean explained. "They say Wednesday, and it's Monday."

"I only wear underwear to bed," Alison responded, getting up from the table to make toast. She pulled a piece of bread from its plastic sleeping bag and slid it into the toaster. When the toast popped up, she added, "I'm just wearing them right now because I'm polite." Then she applied a heavy layer of butter to her toast. Jean scowled and changed the subject. Even with a scowl, Alison thought her mom was pretty. Alison thought she was prettiest of all in the mornings without makeup, the way she was at that moment—her long blond hair wrapped tight in a towel, exposing the longness of her neck, and Jean's tan face, the perfect canvas for her hazel eyes. Alison once asked her mother why she wore so much makeup. Jean told her that it made her "feel nice."

"But what does how you look have to do with how you feel?" Alison had asked her.

"How you look *reflects* how you feel," Jean responded. But Alison thought she had it backward.

"That's an awful lot of butter, Ali."

"You're a lot of butter," Alison replied.

Jean scrunched up her face. "That doesn't make sense."

"You don't make sense," Alison said while putting Tabasco sauce on top of the butter on the top of the toast. Then she licked the butter from the knife, put it in the sink, and sat back down at the table with her spicy toast.

"You're going to give yourself a stroke," Jean said.

Alison shrugged. Bob barked.

"Okay, David, I'll feed you," Jean told Bob.

She had renamed Bob, David, five years ago when Alison's dad left. It seemed to Alison that her mother was renaming the dog after her long-lost dad to take his place. So when people mentioned David, well, Jean just thought of that dog and how nice it was to have someone to talk to, protect her, and sleep next to. But Jean told Alison and her older sister, Sarah, that it was the dog's middle name and that it was what he wanted Jean to call him, sort of like a nickname. Alison couldn't remember the dog ever having a middle name, especially one that was the same as her dad's. But Jean insisted on it so vehemently that she didn't argue. Alison and Sarah still called their dog Bob. And their mom called him David. The dog just began answering to both.

Bob was an ugly dog, not one breed but many breeds that were unrecognizable and didn't match. He had three legs and a tongue that didn't fit his mouth. But a long time ago, when David first brought the dog home, he told Alison and Sarah their new dog was a retired police dog. They both agreed that he was really cool, especially when David told them the dog's leg had been blown off while he was "on the job."

"But how come he's so dirty?" Sarah had asked.

"He's been living ... sort of *undercover* in a pretty scary neighborhood. The policeman I talked to said that it was going to be too difficult for him to work on the force with only three legs, so I agreed to take him." But he told that story a long time ago when Sarah and Alison were too young not to trust their father.

****

Every morning for the past five years, Sarah had woken up angry. Not grumpy. Not *on the wrong side of the bed*. She woke up with a fiery, pulsating knot of anger breathing hate in her chest because that son of a bitch left her in the middle of that dried-up town to either take care of her family or let them go crazy. Sarah knew it was the opinion of most that she did the latter much better than the former. Each day that her father did not either explain or return, her anger intensified. The only way she could get rid of it briefly was to run as hard and as fast as she could for as long as her short, pear-shaped body would allow.

Sarah slapped a blood-filled mosquito into the sweat and rain-covered skin behind her right ear. She was halfway through her morning run, coming up on the edge of the small town, the line where it turned from trees taller than houses and houses as old as trees to nothing but flat farms of cows and corn but nothing of any color—just brown and yellow land and brown and yellow animals. She touched the last tree and turned around. On her way back, the old houses, faded, peeling, slapped in their faces by the rain and kicked in their balls by the mud, stood as they always did, slightly keeled over, grimacing, their cracked and crooked steps resembling the smile of an old man with wooden teeth. Every house in Jasper County looked like this. Even Sarah's house looked like this.

Trenton is an ugly little town, she thought, especially on that particular morning when a group of collaborating clouds sneakily covered up and almost got away with murdering the sun. As Sarah ran over the patchwork of grass and dirt along the curb's upper lip, the rain guiltily stopped to help the sun up. That sun weakly rose and wrapped herself in a stiff, heavy blanket of humidity. It was then that Sarah realized why those clouds wanted the sun dead. The sky turned from gray to pink. Leftover raindrops slid from the fingers of tree branches. Puffs of dirt stuck to and then dried, stuck to and then dried on Sarah's thick bare legs. She smelled the worms tanning in the heat as they weakly slid one another to get through the first layer of hardening mud. Sarah began to get tired. Her legs felt shaky and burned. Her knee bones clicked under skin and muscle. But the hardest part was always her favorite part, the part where she didn't think she could possibly run any more, but she did. She ran faster. Faster. Until she felt like she was flying. She grew wings, or so it seemed, and flew home.

She opened the front door and knew immediately that she had interrupted her mom's conversation with the television set. Jean was pretty heavily involved in a dialogue with Regis and Kathy. Sarah heard Kathy ask Regis a question and her mom answer. Then her mom laughed and answered Regis's question to Kathy.

Like Bob's name, this was just another one of the things that changed in their home after Sarah's dad left. The small television set became a member of the family. And it took a place in many of Jean's conversations. The most confusing were the conversations at the dinner table. Jean would take a bite of her mashed potatoes and suddenly say something like "She's right, ya know." Then Sarah had to follow her mother's eyes to find out if she was talking to Sarah, Alison, or Tim Allen. If Jean was alone for more than two hours, she'd talk to anything—kitchen utensils, the windows, the coffee table. Sarah had walked in on her talking to each of the above when her mother thought no one was around.

"What are you guys talking about?" Sarah asked her mom as she walked into the kitchen and motioned to the small television set by the toaster.

"Oh …" Jean chuckled. "Kathy asked if we wanted to see a picture of her new love seat."

"What'd you say?"

"Well, Reeg said no." Jean rolled her eyes and shook her head back and forth. "But I said yes."

"Did she show you?"

Jean let out a loud burst of laughter. "Of course she showed me! She never listens to Regis!"

"That's true," Sarah said and kissed her mom on the forehead. Then she followed the smell of cigarette smoke to the bathroom where Alison sat on the counter next to the sink and brushed her teeth. Up down. Spit. Smoke. Left right. Spit. Smoke. Up down. Ash. Smoke. Rinse. Repeat. Sarah watched Alison spit one final time and flick her cigarette into the toilet. Then Alison took a swig of coffee, swished it around in her mouth, and spit it at the drain as if it were mouthwash.

"Ahhhh."

"Isn't that a little counterproductive?" Sarah asked, already knowing Alison's answer was going to be as ridiculous as her mother's one-way conversation taking place in the kitchen.

"If you call multitasking counterproductive," Alison answered. Alison picked two teeth that Sarah assumed were totally at random and flossed in between them. Then she looked into the mirror and smiled. The girl in the mirror with hair clumped in places and rough and matted in others who had not yet wiped the excess toothpaste from her mouth smiled back. This was the way Alison would stay. No makeup or extraordinary measures. Dirty, untouched, and completely beautiful. Alison was as genuine on the outside as she was on the inside.

"Well," Sarah said, waving away a line of smoke crawling through the air toward her, "when you are done mixing cancer and cleanliness, let me know. I want to shower."

"Go right ahead," Alison said, hopping down from the counter and leaving the bathroom. "Try to scrub off some of that negativity while you're in there … will ya?"

Even crazier to Sarah than her mother renaming the dog and talking with things that couldn't talk back was her sister's unwavering sense of optimism. Alison still loved their dad with her entire heart; she thought his reason for leaving was one of great secret importance, like the so-called identity of their dog. Sarah just thought he left them for something bigger, better, or easier.

Sarah peeled off her clothes and stepped over the lip of the tub. She turned on the water, which hit her skin weakly and without much warmth. Still it drove the dirt down her skin and around the drain between her feet. Her skin accepted the temperature and pressure with an appreciative shiver. It was the type of shiver that felt good, like the one before a pee or a sneeze. And she sang the first song that came into her head. "Hey, little girl, is your daddy home?"

When Alison barged in and riffled through the drawers for something, she added, "Did he go away and leave you all alone?"

"I got a bad desire," Sarah sang.

"Oh, oh, oh. I'm on fire," Alison sang.

"Tell me now, baby, is he good to you?" Sarah sang.

"Can he do to you the things that I do?" Alison sang.

"I can take you higher," Sarah sang.

But Alison left the bathroom before it was her turn again. Sarah sang, lathered, rinsed, and repeated. She could hear Bob drinking from the toilet bowl with the cigarette still floating in it. Jean knocked on the bathroom door.

"I'm going to work!" she yelled. "I love you."

"Love you too!" Sarah yelled back.

****

"That's what you're wearing, huh?" Sarah looked at Alison's shirt and rolled her eyes. It was, at the very least, approximately six years old. It was a red-and-orange tie-dyed T-shirt with a pocket sewn in the middle labeled "stuff." Six years ago, Sarah thought it looked a little young for Alison. But nothing in Alison's closet was newer than two or three years old. Most of her clothing was bought sometime in between her sophomore and her senior years of high school. In fact, most of her clothing could tell you horror stories about the cold and dusty floors of boys' rooms Alison had forced them to sleep on throughout her later teens—that is, if thread could talk.

Alison saw no need to buy new clothes after her sixteenth birthday when she told Sarah that she had wished she would not grow another inch taller as she blew out her birthday candles. The very next day, her wish came true. She had stopped, just a hair over five feet eleven inches. The following year, she told Sarah she wished for a pair of boobs. But the candles probably just laughed their fiery little faces off.

Jean never saw the need for Alison to wear a bra. And neither did Alison. When Alison began fooling around with boys, they either didn't care or didn't notice.

****

As Alison and Sarah walked together to Casey's General Store that Monday morning, like they had done every Monday morning since their dad disappeared, Sarah knew they looked nothing like sisters. They didn't even appear related. Sarah looked like her dad. Her figure was the exact opposite of her sister's. She was short, curved, and pale. Her hair was not straight but not curly. Her face was like her father's— brown eyes and round cheeks. Alison looked like a taller version of her mom with features that pointed and limbs that were long and straight.

It was on her eighteenth birthday that their dad bought Alison her first scratch ticket and she won a dollar. Just one dollar. She made him go with her every Monday that followed. When he left, Alison forced Sarah to go in his place.

****

The bell on the door made a jingling sound when Sarah opened it. The inside of the store was the same temperature as the outside of the store, which was about eighty-five degrees. And the humidity made everything inside it sweat—the gray-colored linoleum, the four red Formica booths and their benches, and the cans, boxes, and bags on the shelves. Even the magazines looked wet. Josie, the woman behind the counter, was visibly sweating. Layers of her makeup melted in little lines down her face. Her hair, however, was unaffected. It remained the size and color of a pumpkin as it had for probably all fifty or so years of her life as far as Sarah could figure. Josie was popping the gum inside her pink-frosted lips that sparkled every time the sun hit them as she talked with Bob.

Bob was the policeman who hung out pretty much all day and all night at the general store. He was the only police officer Alison and Sarah knew when they got their little police dog. So they named their dog after him. A long time ago, when Alison and Sarah still believed their dog was a retired cop, they asked Officer Bob if he knew about their undercover police dog. He had scratched his mustache and said he didn't. But they figured the poor guy probably didn't get to do any undercover jobs—not in Jasper County, anyway. Nothing interesting ever seemed to happen in Jasper County. They also figured it would be in their new dog's best interest not to discuss his past.

It wasn't until years later that Sarah and Alison realized Officer Bob didn't spend all his time at Casey's to protect it from being robbed. He spent every waking moment there so that he could be close to Josie. She was the woman he had loved since they went to high school together, the woman he had tried to impress by becoming a police officer in the first place. Even after the two of them married, Bob still spent every day trying to impress her. In Sarah's opinion, it was pathetic. But Alison told Sarah she thought it was beautiful.

"Hiya," Josie said.

"How are you ladies today?" Bob added, twisting one side of his auburn mustache with a click pen. When Bob and Josie stood next to one another, there was a combined scent of stale coffee, bubblegum, and Aqua Net. Sarah always had to breathe through her mouth.

"We're good. Can I have twenty Megabucks please and two grilled cheese with fries and coffee … oh and this," Alison said as she grabbed a bag of Cheetos from the rack next to the beef jerky and threw it on the counter. "And a chocolate doughnut," she added.

"You bet," Josie replied, clicking on the register with her pink nails. Bob went around the counter and stood next to Josie as she selected a stack of glossy scratch tickets. "Which ones look lucky to you, Bob?" Josie asked her husband.

Bob smiled as he pulled twenty tickets from the bottom of the pile. "These are the lucky ones," he said, handing them to Josie.

Josie handed them to Sarah, along with Alison's chocolate doughnut. "Grab your coffee, and I'll bring your sandwiches and fries over in a minute. You want Tabasco, right, Alison?"

"You know it, Josie," Alison said, grabbing her Cheetos and heading toward a booth where she sat down.

She eats like an unsupervised six-year-old, Sarah thought as she paid Josie, grabbed the doughnut, and went to pour her and Alison's coffees. She blew on both coffees as she walked toward the table Alison had already dumped her Cheetos all over. Although Sarah was only two years older than Alison, she was always doing things like blowing on her hot coffee to cool it down. It wasn't that she thought Alison was vulnerable or naive, like a lot of people probably did. She just always wanted to take care of her little sister.

"Why does Josie always have Bob give us our tickets?" Sarah asked Alison as she set the coffees down and threw Alison's doughnut at her. "He treats her like she doesn't have any arms. Plus, he treats me like I am four years old."

"I don't think he treats you like a four-year-old. And Josie loves him dearly," Alison said, taking a large bite of her doughnut. Then she reached across the table and grabbed a scratch ticket from Sarah's hand. "Besides, we always win. Maybe Bob's psychic or something."

"Yeah, probably."

"Are you being sarcastic or are you really agreeing with me because—"

"Wipe your mouth, Ali," Sarah interrupted. "It's covered in chocolate."

"You are," Alison said and started scratching the silver flakes from her ticket with a penny.

"You look like you've been eating poop."

"You do," Alison said. Then she looked at Sarah. Sarah looked back at her. "Fiiiiine," Alison said dramatically. She slid the back of her arm across the bottom half of her face.

"Sorry to interrupt," Josie said as she approached the table and set down the sandwiches and fries.

"Thanks, Josie," Sarah said.

"Hey, Josie, do I have chocolate on my face," Alison asked, looking up at her.

"A little."

"Does it bother you?"

"Not in the slightest."

"Thank you, Josie," Alison said. Then she looked at Sarah and smiled widely.

Sarah rolled her eyes. "She's being polite, dipshit."

Josie shrugged and left the two of them alone.

"Oh! Oh, hey! I can't believe I almost forgot!" Alison exclaimed. "I think …" And it actually looked like she was thinking when she said, "I saw Dad at the video store yesterday."

As was usually the case when Alison started a conversation, Sarah was doubtful but curious. Alison always thought she saw Dad somewhere. And although it was completely ridiculous, it was, at least, fitting that she would bring this up here, the very place she and her dad had spent so many mornings together.

"What did he look like this time?" Sarah asked, licking the french fry salt off her fingers and grabbing another ticket.

"The same. Maybe a little skinnier," Alison said as she leaned toward Sarah and lowered the volume of her voice, as if to secure the secrecy of their conversation. She added quietly, "Maybe he works there." She didn't wait for Sarah to comment. Or if she did, she didn't wait long enough.

"He was wearing a blue shirt like an employee. And he was holding a lot of movies. You know, I'll bet—" She was beginning to get all worked up. And when she got all worked up, she didn't pause to swallow or breathe or blink.

"Ali," Sarah interrupted. "Even if it was Dad, which it probably wasn't, and he did work at the video store, which he probably doesn't ..." There was a fresh pot of anger brewing beneath Sarah's skin. She could feel her face turning the pinkish color of a slightly acidic strip of litmus paper. She couldn't stop herself from saying, "Our dad is an asshole coward. And he is long gone from this place."

"Fuck you," Alison said, shaking her head back and forth defiantly. "You don't know why he left and when he's coming back, and he's not an asshole, and he's not a coward. You're the fucking asshole, you know." She smacked her hands down on the table, making the Cheetos on the table jump in unison.

"There's no such thing as a *good* bye, Sarah. Byes are never fucking good," Alison added, putting one of her hands over one of Sarah's hands.

Sarah watched the tears welling in her sister's eyes. One escaped and rolled down her cheek. For Alison, anger was a transitional state. As soon as something made her angry, her anger immediately transformed itself into sadness. She couldn't stay angry at anyone or anything for more than a few seconds. But she cried often and easily.

This made Sarah even angrier.

"I forgot to give you your hot sauce," Josie said softly as she approached the table. She delicately set the Tabasco bottle down in front of Alison and gave her a little squeeze on the shoulder afterward. Then she promptly left.

"I hate it when you cry. You always cry."

"I can't help it," Alison said. And as she did, another tear slipped out.

"I know you can't. And that's why I hate him. Because he makes you cry."

"No, he doesn't. You are right. I always cry. And you don't hate him. You just think you do." She breathed a heavy sigh and gave Sarah a sympathetic look. Then she smiled.

This made Sarah smile.

Sarah's reaction seemed to satisfy Alison, who immediately covered her food in hot sauce and then nodded her head assertively. As she took a bite of her grilled cheese, she seemed to reassure herself by saying very softly, "It could have been Dad at the video store." She carefully enunciated every syllable. Little cheesy bread sparks went parachuting from her mouth. She slid the back of her arm across her lips like a chalkboard eraser. She watched Sarah watch her as she did it. Then she stuck out her tongue.

Alison dropped her head and went back to scratching a shiny circle on her scratch ticket. She went through four tickets in silence when all of a sudden, she froze, midscratch, and yelled, "Jack-mother-fucking-pot!"

Josie stopped right in the middle of a "Have a nice day." "Have a nice …" was all she got to say to a middle-aged guy who was holding hands with a six-pack of RC Cola.

Sarah held her excitement and leaned across the table over Alison's scratch ticket to examine her claim.

"Hey, good job," she said.

"Day," Josie finished.

"Told you those were the lucky ones," Bob called.

Josie smiled and popped her gum.

"We just won twenty *dollars*!" Alison screamed. Her thick lips stretched into a closed smile like two pregnant caterpillars snoozing on an imaginary hammock.

"They know," Sarah assured her.

"Yessss!" Alison yelled, waving a triumphant fist in the air.

The guy with the six-pack of RC looked at her and politely said, "Congratulations, miss."

"Thanks, dude," she answered, throwing a thumbs-up with her left hand while taking a bite of her grilled cheese with her right. And just like that, they were back to their lives without their father.

CHAPTER 2

Mother Nature
never had any children.
She was actually barren—
adopted the rain
and wind
and snow
out of sympathy
for children with disabilities
and abnormalities
who no one else wanted
until we all realized
we couldn't live without them.

The restaurant that Alison and Sarah worked in, Doug's, was the only restaurant in town, unless you counted the Casey's General Store or the bar or the ice-cream shop. It was planted in a square of dirt on the edge of town that Sarah ran away from every morning. This was the side that was shoved up, under, and alongside the highway so that the people who lived on this side of town had to listen to everyone passing them by as they sat on their front porches.

On the outside, the restaurant was nothing more than a brown box with a neon sign. But on the inside, the walls were painted a Mary Kay pink, while the floors were tiled in different shades of blue and spread about in no identifiable pattern. The furniture looked like it had been cheaply and hurriedly purchased from various garage sales. Some chairs were wood, others plastic, and the rest were a suspicious hodgepodge of both. None were the same size. So when people sat down at a table, some invariably looked up, while others were forced to look down, instead of right at one another. If Doug were anybody but Doug, his employees would have been forced to admire his childlike effort, maybe even applaud the independently imaginative and audacious endeavor of creating and running a business. But Doug was Doug. He was a narcissistic, pushy, pudgy curmudgeon, a spirit squasher, and a Scrooge McDuck.

As Alison clocked in, she could feel and smell Doug's chili dog breath over her shoulder.

"You're late, Alison," he said after silently standing behind her for thirty full seconds.

"I'm sorry," she turned around and told him.

"Let's just try to get though the day without soliciting a search party for your old man."

"Sure," she said, tucking a thick square of folded-up flyers into her pocket so that they were not noticeable. His fat fingers drummed the wall next to her face and left quarter-sized grease prints on the pink paint.

"And quit using the copy machine. You owe me paper."

"I'm sorry twice," Alison replied. Alison didn't hate Doug like the rest of her coworkers. She just hated his pig breath. It made her feel like she was being forced to eat pork, which she didn't eat. Nor did she eat beef or chicken or fish or anything that "took poops." When Alison said she didn't eat shit, she meant it quite literally.

"You look like shit," Doug said to her. Then he wiped little pieces of reddish-brown goo from his fingers onto his tan corduroys. As he waddled toward his office in the back of the restaurant, the rivets on his corduroys zipped against one another. Luke, Alison's coworker, neighbor, and friend (but not necessarily in that order), said that Doug probably thought of it as a round of applause. That was why he was always walking away after one-liners. Why else would a three-hundred-pound man wear corduroys in the middle of the summer?

It was obvious Luke didn't hate Doug so much as he was afraid of him. But Luke was afraid of a lot of things.

Ali says you guys won twenty today. Can I take your tables?" Luke asked, walking toward Sarah.

"If they look poor," Sarah replied.

"Bitch," he said. He was smiling, which he meant he was completely kidding.

But Sarah narrowed her eyes and raised her hand toward him.

"Sorry, sorry, sorry!" Luke shouted as he went sprinting toward the bar. He hid behind his brother, his protector, James, the bartender.

"What are you doing?" James looked over his shoulder and asked Luke.

"I called Sarah a bitch. Now she's going to hit me," Luke said in a shaky, high-pitched voice to the back of James's neck. Luke's voice was two octaves higher than Sarah's, Alison's, or James's and three when he was excited or frightened.

James laughed and took a step to the right. Luke moved with him. Then James took a step to the left. Luke moved with him again. James took another step left. And Luke bolted toward the kitchen.

"You're afraid of a girl?" James smiled as he called to the back of Luke's head. James's smile was awkwardly rigid, as if it were drawn with a ruler on a grid. It was genuine and precise, as was his short blond hair, his oxfords, buttons, belts, and so on. But then again, James was a very precise person.

"*I am a girl,*" Luke yelled back over the fast clicking sound of his cowboy boots on the tiled floor. Then he barreled through the kitchen door.

"*And* he's your brother," Alison said to James.

"Actually he's your cousin," Sarah corrected.

"Potayto, potahto," James replied.

****

Technically, Luke wasn't James's brother. Luke was the illegitimate son of James's mom's sister, who was now in prison for running a meth lab in her basement. James and Luke had grown up together as brothers. They referred to one another as "brother," which had to be explained in great detail at first because Luke's dad, whom he had only met once, was black. Luke had gotten all of his dad's yin and none of his mom's yang, pigmentally speaking. Luckily the town was small and the story only needed to be told about five times before everyone knew at least bits and pieces of it and stopped asking.

****

Alison knew Luke would have been safer had he stayed behind the bar and taken his chances at being hit by a girl. In the kitchen, the overly competitive cooks, Big Joe and Little Joe, were in the middle of a food fight. Shards of carrots and green grape pellets went flying through the air. Luke took cover behind the old electric dishwasher and under the sink. Little Joe wasn't nearly as small as Luke. Everyone called him Little Joe because the other Joe, Big Joe, was so enormous.

When Alison came into the kitchen only seconds after Luke, he was nowhere to be found. She poured herself a coffee as she glanced around the room at all the possible places Luke could be hiding.

"My coleslaw is ten times better than yours!" Big Joe shouted, chucking a handful of hot french fries at Little Joe. Little Joe shielded himself with a pan lid and threw back an entire onion as hard as he could.

"You don't even use horseradish!" Little Joe shouted back. The onion barely missed Big Joe's big head.

"That's it!" Big Joe screamed. He pulled a wrench out of his pocket and started waving it in the air. Little Joe laughed and grabbed a knife.

"Use your own knife. That one's mine!" Big Joe screamed. "You know I don't want anyone touching my things. That's why I ain't married!"

Alison spotted poor, scared Luke, who had really been scared his whole life. And the position he put himself in was strangely familiar to anyone who had heard the story about when the police came for his mother.

****

He was in that exact position, though he was in his bedroom closet instead of under a sink. He told Alison he bit his knee so hard it bled. He told James he had no idea his mother was running a meth lab in the basement. She had told Luke not to go downstairs because there were monsters down there. He never did go downstairs. He said he was genuinely scared. He thought the cops were coming to take him to jail for playing with Barbies. His mother told him that it was against the law for boys to play with dolls. And now he was going to jail for it.

"Luke, honey. Please! Luke, where are you?" his mother screamed as she was being handcuffed. But Luke wouldn't come out from his hiding spot. He thought if the policemen didn't look under the bed, they wouldn't find his dolls and he and his mom would be safe.

"Luke!" his mother shrieked. "Please come out! Mommy has to kiss you good-bye. I love you, sweetheart. Let Mommy say good-bye to you!" But he didn't come out and she never kissed him good-bye. There he hid in that closet, just a seven-year-old, half the size of all the other seven-year-olds, breathing into his hands with his eyes locked shut.

When the cops found him forty-five minutes later, they didn't ask him anything about the Barbies under his bed. They just asked him about his mother and what she kept in the basement. "I only play with trucks," he told them in the deepest voice he could muster. "And I am not afraid of monsters," he lied.

****

Shortly after Alison spotted Luke's hiding place under the sink, she heard his piercing scream, which must have been loud enough to be heard all the way at the bar because Sarah and James came running through the door. It was a quarter after ten, which meant James had been in the middle of turning the different-colored liquor bottles label facing forward with one pinky finger's distance between each bottle. It was not something Doug had asked him to do—although Doug did ask his employees to do some pretty ridiculous things from time to time. It was just something James did because he needed order and he needed to do certain things at certain times. James's watch was missing from his wrist, which meant he had taken it off to save the place between the liquor bottles that were and weren't done.

"I am under the sink!" Luke cried when he heard Sarah and James rush into the kitchen. Big Joe and Little Joe stood frozen, kitchen knives in hand. Little Joe looked at James and put his knife down. Big Joe looked toward the cowboy boots sticking out from under the sink and put his knife down.

"Sorry," Little Joe told James.

"Come out from under that sink!" Big Joe called. "Me and Little Joe are just messing around."

Luke got up slowly. He smiled weakly and uncovered his head.

"God, Luke, you are not afraid of anything, are you?" Alison said sarcastically.

James elbowed Alison in the rib cage.

"Elbow me again and I'll mess up all the liquor bottles you just straightened," she told him.

"I am not afraid of anything either," James told her. He winked at her before he walked back out into the restaurant.

****

At ten thirty, Alison flipped the sign from closed to open and waited by the front door. She stood next to that open sign and scanned the parking lot for cars, bikes, any sign of movement. She wanted to be at the front door to greet the first table, to welcome them in, make them fall in love with their entire dining experience. She fidgeted with the mood ring her dad had given her when she was nine. It now only fit halfway down her pinky. And it was a greenish-yellow color, which meant that she was happy.

This was the only color anyone had ever seen it.

She pulled her hands down to her sides as two teenagers walked through the front door.

"Hi!" she screamed excitedly and immediately handed them two menus.

One of them took a step back. The other one looked from the pocket on Alison's shirt to her smile. He smiled back.

"We're not eating. We just wanted to see if you're hiring," the one who took a step back explained.

"Oh," Alison said disappointedly. "No." Her smile brightened back up. "But if you want to eat, I can get you something." Her smile stretched up, up, and away. "My name is Alison." She extended the menus out once again.

"No, thank you," one of the teenagers said, tugging on his friend's arm and pulling him toward the door.

"Hang on a second," Alison said, looking over both shoulders twice. She pulled the square of folded papers out of her back pocket, unfolded it, took one, handed it to one of the boys, and then folded up the rest and put them back into her pocket. "Have you seen the man in this picture?" she asked, pointing at the middle of the paper she had given the boy. The boy holding the paper looked at the picture and shook his head no. The boy not holding the paper looked at the door. "Hey!" Alison said, snapping her fingers at the boy looking at the door. "You have to actually fucking look at the picture," she said, taking the paper from the boy who was holding it and putting it in the other boy's face. He looked at the paper.

"No, sorry," he stammered.

"Wait! I'm sorry. Keep it, please," she said, handing it back to the first boy. "Show it to your friends and enemies."

He took the paper and walked toward the door with his friend.

"Thanks. Have a really great day," she said to the backs of their heads as they walked out the door.

After several more minutes of waiting by the front door and no one else coming in, Alison joined Luke, James, and Sarah in a game of hot potato with an actual hot potato.

James tossed the potato at Luke.

Luke caught it, screamed, and then dropped it. "*Hot potato!*"

"Hey, throw it back!" James called.

Luke picked up the potato with his shirt over his hand and heaved it back at James with his best underhand.

"What are you guys playing?" Trisha, the last staff member to arrive, asked as she set her bag down and joined the circle.

"Kickball," Sarah answered.

"Don't be so fucking mean," Alison scolded Sarah as she caught the potato James threw at her.

"Fun," Trisha said. "Where's the ball?"

Luke laughed as he tucked his shirt back in and smoothed it. Luke was always tucking his shirt in to make sure that everyone could see his massive metal belt buckle—as if everyone didn't already know he wanted to be a cowboy by the fact that he wore cowboy boots every day. Even in summer.

****

Trisha was a large, freckled flower of a girl who smelled like baby powder and apple juice. She was doughnut-hole sized. Her bangs were curled every morning and hair-sprayed into a perfect immovable loop. The rest of her hair, bouncy and brown, flipped like an upside-down umbrella at the bottom. She made her face up in all the colors of Easter Sunday. She was particularly fond of shirts with kittens either sewn or painted on them by someone at a craft table. She wore jeans that fit snuggly around the equator of her round stomach. She wore either a pink or a yellow belt through the loops of her jeans to give her body the effect of a globe being squeezed too tight. And when she sneezed, all the continents shook. She lacked both exercise and sunlight.

Trisha was a walking advertisement against homeschooling. She thought that China was in Europe and that Christopher Columbus threw the Boston Tea Party for the Indians to welcome them to America.

"At least she knows Boston is in the United States," Alison had tried to defend Trisha. Although Trisha later asked her, "If they are all so united, why does Canada have a different flag?"

All her coworkers were crossing their fingers for her not to homeschool her own kids. It was no wonder to them that her three-year-old, Jennifer, acted like a cat or that her six-year-old, Terrence, got Santa Claus and Jesus confused. Alison knew for a fact that last Christmas Terrence stayed up all night just to catch a glimpse of God's only son sliding down the chimney.

****

By the time Trisha figured out her coworkers weren't playing kickball, Little Joe stuck his head out of the kitchen door and told the waitstaff that Doug was coming out of his office. Everyone immediately pretended to be working. Alison grabbed a few bottles of ketchup off of the shelf and began to marry them. James went back to the bar to turn all the dollar bills in the cash register the same way. Luke helped Alison with the ketchup. Trisha grabbed the two things closest to her, a lemon and a ladle.

"What *are* you doing?" Doug demanded as he approached his employees.

"Washing my hands," Trisha blurted.

"With a lemon and a big spoon?"

"It's a ladle," Sarah corrected.

"What?" Doug snapped.

"It's called a ladle, not a big spoon."

"I know what it's called," he said, waving his hand in front of Sarah's face. "What is it that you are doing?"

"I'm watching Trisha wash her hands."

"Go clean the front door, smartass," he replied.

"And you go help her," he told Luke. Then he snatched the lemon and ladle from Trisha's hands.

****

After Luke and Sarah had finished cleaning the front door, an old couple walked through it, hanging on to one another's arms, squinting at "today's special." The sign said, "Kids eat free." But it didn't appear that either one of them could make it out.

"Table for two?" Alison asked, slightly out of breath because she had sprinted from the bar to the front door when she saw it being opened.

"No, there's going to be a bunch of us."

"How many?"

"I don't know, ten or twenty."

"Which one?" Sarah asked, stepping out from behind Alison.

Alison shot Sarah a look. *Don't you dare patronize this cute old couple.*

"What?" the old man asked, wrinkling up his wrinkles.

"Ten *or* twenty," Sarah repeated her question, emphasizing the word *or*.

The old man looked agitated.

"Right." He nodded his head. "Ten or twenty," he repeated his answer.

"We'll start with a table set for ten," Sarah said. It may have come out a bit more condescending than she meant. But Alison knew her sister didn't care. Sarah wasn't that type of considerate.

The old woman looked puzzled. Alison looked at the old man and then at Sarah. "We are meeting the bingo club," the old lady said. But the way she said it made it sound like a question.

"Wait here, please," Sarah commanded.

"Yes," Alison said. Then she looked around for Doug. The coast was clear. She put a hand on the old lady's shoulder. "And please put this up at your bingo club." Alison handed the lady another flyer from her back pocket. Then she smiled and followed Sarah toward the back of the restaurant.

The old couple stood there and tried to make out what the special board said. "Something is free," Alison heard the old lady say to the old man.

"What is it?" he asked her.

"I can't tell."

James, Luke, and Trisha helped Alison push tables together in Luke's section, while Sarah went to the back to tell the cooks that there would soon be a large party coming in.

"Ah, what's free?" Luke imitated the cute old man. "Food? Is food free today?" he said, talking with his lips over his teeth. "You guys got apple sauce? 'Cause we don't have teeth." Luke laughed at himself. He already did look a little bit like an old man anyway, being so small and hairless.

"Shh! What if they can hear you?" Trisha said in a whisper.

"Honey, they couldn't hear an atom bomb," Luke said, putting his hands on his hips.

"What?" Trisha asked, leaning her good ear toward Luke. He repeated himself.

Then Trisha said, "Well, Jesus can hear you. And he can hear Adam's bomb too."

Luke looked from Trisha's somber face to James's and Alison's expressions of puzzled amusement. Alison could tell by James's face that he was trying not to laugh by counting the polka dots on Trisha's shirt, which made it look like he was staring at her boobs.

"What do you guys think? Can Jesus hear Adam's bomb?" Luke said, taking his hands off his hips and throwing them up in the air where Alison assumed he thought Jesus lived. Alison started laughing. But James continued to hold it in.

"What's so funny?" Trisha asked. "Was Adam's bomb a joke bomb or something?"

With that, the redness left James's face and the laughter came exploding out of his mouth.

"Oh, Trisha," Luke said and kissed her on the forehead. "I love you so much."

Trisha beamed.

"I love you too," she said and threw her two huge sausage arms around him.

Whoever it was that came up with the saying "Ignorance is bliss" must have known someone like Trisha, Alison thought.

****

The old couple must have given up on reading the sign because the old man grabbed the old lady's arm and said, "Let's go sit down." He led her to a table set for four.

"Your table is going to be over there," Sarah said as she approached the old couple and motioned toward the tables that had been pushed together and set.

"Can I have a Bloody Mary?" the old lady asked. "What are you going to have, Herbert? I'll have a Bloody Mary, and he'll have—"

"Ma'am, I am not your server. And this is not your table. Your table is going to be over there," Sarah said, motioning again to the tables that had been pushed together. Herbert was looking over the menu as the old lady began to get up. She grunted a little and stopped to breathe, resting her hand on the table. When she was about halfway upright, she let out a tiny, squeaky fart that smelled like eggs. Herbert put down his menu and followed the old lady's lead. Sarah walked slowly beside them as they shuffled toward their table. Although Alison could smell that fart from four tables away, she could tell that her sister's patience was about to expire, so she stepped in to walk with the couple for the rest of the way. She linked arms right in between the two old-timers as if they were family members. She walked in, through, and out of the old lady's fart cloud without so much as batting an eye.

Sarah should have stuck with the cute old couple, Alison thought as she watched Sarah begin to take the order for a table of six. She saw one of them hand Sarah a laminated card with what she assumed was a list of ingredients that they were not allowed to eat.

"None of you can have these?" Sarah asked.

"Just us," a heavy lady said, pointing to another heavy lady and an extremely heavy man.

The skinniest fat lady asked Sarah if the soups were refillable.

"I'm sorry, no," Sarah said. She turned her head away from her table to hold in a laugh.

Alison giggled as she watched her sister unsuccessfully try to muffle a heavy sigh by pursing her lips and blowing air out her nose. *That's what you get for being afraid of a little fart.*

"I will talk with our cook about your problem," Sarah said after she pulled herself together and turned back around to face her customers. Big blank faces stared back at her. "About your diet," she corrected. Less blank, more confused faces. "Um … your laminated card," Sarah said, walking away before one of them wanted to argue that their eating habits were neither a problem nor a diet.

Alison stopped eavesdropping just in time to notice Doug walking out the front door with his car keys. As soon as he was outside, Alison yelled, "Woohoo! Copy machine time," and ran to his office to make copies of her flyers.

CHAPTER 3

Jean and David were married by a judge
in a sticky wooden room.
No wedding dress or flower girl
except Jean.
Just two hippies fresh out of high school
signing their I dos
as God sat watching from the witness stand.
Jean hopped on the back of a motorcycle
that dragged cans and toilet paper up the driveway
of their new house.
Together
they fed each other cake
and filled plastic cups
with Miller Lite.
Jean's new name
wrapped around her
and her new husband on brown shag carpet.
David mouthed all the words to Bob Dylan's
"Love Minus Zero" in Jean's ear.
Two kids and a tire swing later,
Jean made egg-salad sandwiches.
David got rid of his bike
but kept his beard

to catch bread crumbs
like spiders catch bugs—
lucky bread crumbs,
with a life span that begins in a plastic bag
and ends on Jean's bottom lip
as he kissed her good-bye.
On his way to work,
five miles under the speed limit
in his brand-new used car,
AM radio softly paralleled the pavement,
cigarette burned in the ashtray,
while Jean put her children to bed,
cleaned the house,
did the laundry, and watched *Laverne and Shirley.*
A few years later, Jean got a part-time job
doing more cleaning,
and David started working overtime.
Drove away in a noisy Oldsmobile,
radio blaring,
left Jean at the window staring
at her bird feeders and begonias
thinking love just doesn't keep
the way leftovers do
and things that are left over
never taste like new
anyway.

On the day he left her,
Jean called her best friend.
Crying all over the phone,

they could barely hear one another,
both red and puffy and wet
telling each other not to think
about what comes next
to nothing.
There is always something,
but neither of them could stop crying,
and neither of them could figure out
why sometimes your head says everything is all right
when your heart says it's all wrong.
And neither of them
could remember the second verse of
that old Bob Dylan Song.

J ean was standing in the hot laundry room of the Horizon Hotel with her three best friends: Linda, James's mother; Gloria, a tiny Mexican woman; and Boo Boo. Boo Boo was a transvestite, which noone, except all the people in the room at that very minute, knew. Boo Boo bore a striking resemblance to Dorothy from the *Golden Girls* when she was dressed a woman. Jean assumed the resemblance was still there when *she* changed into a *he* but couldn't be sure since she had never actually met him. Boo Boo unzipped her maids uniform to reveal a freshly waxed chest and the lacey edges of a tissue-stuffed Wonderbra. "My Lord, it's hot in here," she said, interrupting a conversation that Jean and Gloria were having concerning the whereabouts of Jean's missing husband.

"Maybe you put out missing person report," Gloria was saying in her best English to Jean as she loaded up a metal cart with cleaning supplies and toiletries.

"I did file a report. No one took him. He left on his own. Probably to be with someone else."

"He packed a suitcase," Linda explained with her head down. Then she looked at Jean, apologetically, as if she were sorry for supplying proof that Jean's husband left by choice.

"My youngest is determined to find him," Jean said, eyeing the employee bulletin board with one of Alison's flyers taped to it. She heaved a heavy sigh. "Those are all over town, probably lots of towns. She makes new ones every week, sends them anyplace she's got an address for."

"Why he leave and no say anythings?" Gloria asked. She had only been working at the hotel for a few months and was still catching up on what Linda and Boo Boo already knew.

"Well," Jean said slowly, "we never really saw each other much. I guess he felt like he was just leaving that house and not me."

"That is muy tristo."

Boo Boo grabbed a stack of folded white towels. She traced the outline of a heart on the top towel and handed the stack to Jean. Jean smiled. Linda looked back down at the floor but put a hand on Jean's shoulder.

Jean opened the large circular door to a dryer. A blast of warm air hit her in the face. She too unzipped her uniform, but not quite as far as Boo Boo had. Jean decided it was best to change the subject. "I know I wasn't put on this earth to clean up after people, but it sure the hell feels like it," she said, pulling warm white towels out of the machine.

"You ever want to do something else?" Linda asked, looking at the fresh white towels Jean handed her instead of Jean. Linda's pale skin was beginning to look flushed from the heat. This made her hair look even redder.

Linda was the only person Jean had ever seen with actual red hair. Every strand was the color of the skin on a Macintosh apple, and the brightness of her hair made her skin seem the color of paper. Jean guessed that being married to the man she was married to had frightened the color right out of Linda. It was true she was afraid many times for her life and even more for the lives of James and Luke. But it was staying inside that house that kept the color from touching her skin. Her skin was so pale that she looked strange when she wore the color white, like there were loose pieces of her own flesh draped around her. Whenever she was outside in the daylight, she wore big, dark sunglasses and an oversized floppy hat that looked like a flower flipped upside down.

Linda had a tendency to look at the floor so that when she talked, it was like she was talking to a chair leg, which probably made Jean's children wonder, since they had caught their mother talking to a chair leg on more than one occasion. Linda was so quiet even her footsteps didn't make noise. Unlike Jean, she had spent the latter part of her life trying not to be noticed. She could be standing right in front of you washing the dishes and you'd never even notice her unless she dropped one. Even then, you'd probably notice the pattern on the dish before you noticed her. Over the past eight years, Jean and Linda had become closer than the pieces of popcorn you string around a Christmas tree. Jean knew this made Sarah, Alison, James, and Luke feel as though they had two families instead of one.

"Yeah, but what could *I* do?" Jean answered in a defeated tone.

"A million things!" Boo Boo exclaimed. "You can do a million other things."

"Me? No. I can't do much," Jean said, shaking her head from side to side.

"You can do whatever you want," Boo Boo said, poking a large finger into Jean's right shoulder. Jean tried to look up at Boo Boo's face instead of at her Adam's apple.

"I seriously doubt that."

"Well," Boo Boo said confidently, "I like cleaning up after people."

"Que?" Gloria asked curiously.

"I like to make things fresh and nice. I like to look at a room after it is cleaned and say, 'I did a good job here. I did a better job than anyone else could have done,'" Boo Boo explained.

"That is a good feeling," Linda admitted.

"If you were not doing this, what would you do?" Linda asked Jean.

"I don't know," Jean said, pausing for a minute to think. Then she patted a pile of folded towels, looked up, and said, "I would plant flowers and drink wine."

"Well, that *would* be a nice job," Boo Boo commented, nodding her square jaw up and down.

"Wouldn't it?" Jean said dreamily.

"I would do jigsaw puzzles," Linda said. Then she laughed. "And drink wine," she added.

"I would eat Raisinets and watch the ..." Gloria paused and appeared to be looking for the right word. "Como se dice ... birdies?" She looked at Jean for confirmation.

"Yes, birdies," Jean said.

"Well, let me know how much that pays," Boo Boo said, laughing as she opened another dryer.

CHAPTER 4

Given the chance,
James would turn off his brain;
given the chance, he would
resist the urge
to catalogue and count and contain
each action,
emotion,
and thing.
Besides Alison,
counting was the only thing
that made him feel
calm.
She was something
he could count on
to be predictably loyal—
like an equation,
whether he was solving for x,

y,

or

z

or

Love

or you

or me.

James was putting Tabasco sauce into a Bloody Mary that Luke was waiting to take to one of his tables when a customer sitting at the bar yelled something at the television. James glanced over his shoulder at the TV. Then he shook his head and said to Luke, "Two thousand two hundred ninety-seven RBIs. Who would have thought?"

Luke, who probably didn't even know what an RBI was, just answered, "Not me."

The guy at the bar who had yelled at the television looked at James and snapped, "Two thousand two hundred ninety-seven, that ain't right."

"Careerwise," James explained without turning around to face the customer. "I'm pretty sure it's right," he said and handed Luke the Bloody Mary. James wasn't trying to draw attention to himself. He was just making a comment the way people sometimes say, "Nice weather." Regardless, it had begun. Luke didn't leave to deliver the drink to his table. James knew Luke was proud of this part of him. It was one of many parts that was so unlike any parts that made up Luke.

"How do you know?" the guy asked, taking off his Dodgers hat and setting it on the bar.

"I am good with numbers."

"He knows how many licks it takes to get to the Tootsie Pop," Luke added proudly.

"Oh, yeah? How many?" the guy asked, scratching his hat hair and tilting his head.

"Three hundred and thirty-five."

"I don't believe you."

The guy next to the Dodgers fan called out to James, "Hey, James, how much for soup, two cheeseburgers, carrot cake, and a Coke, plus tax?"

"Twenty-three eighty-nine."

The Dodgers fan's mouth fell open. "Hey, I've heard about you," he said suddenly. Then he added, "How much without the soup."

"Twenty sixty-two."

As the guy continued to test James's abilities, he knew the look on his face must have been one-half bored, the other half annoyed because

Alison was looking at him like she wanted to say something but didn't know what. Just staring quietly while biting her lip. He felt like a freak at the circus sideshow—some boy with webbed hands and feet looking back at her through his lonely tank of water.

"Hey, James," she said, walking toward him as if reading his mind. "Can you come help me lift something heavy?"

"Please," he said and winked at her.

"Thank you," she said and smiled.

He smiled back, took off his watch, and set it behind the bar.

"Do you really need me to pick something up?" he asked after he excused himself from his customers at the bar.

"No." She shook her head. "But you're welcome to escort me to a cigarette break," she said, holding out her hand.

"It would be my pleasure," he replied and took her hand in his. He couldn't help but say the number fourteen to himself. It was the number of times they had held hands.

James had never been tested in a hospital or a doctor's office or even on paper by a board of professionals who could put into words the schematics of his brain. It just was that the numbers in his life were all accounted for, like a book of numerical photographs. And whenever he wanted to locate a certain date or time or count, all he had to do was flip backward through them. He had a photographic memory of numbers.

James was the closest Jasper County ever came to producing a celebrity. They considered themselves lucky to have a living, breathing archive for their town, an encyclopedia of deaths and births, someone to keep track of weddings and anniversaries. But those who did not know James like his friends and family knew him only knew this part of him. And most people didn't really take the time to get to know him. They asked irrelevant questions like "What's my license plate number?" or "How many times have I ordered that?" They treated him as if he were a shopping mall Santa Claus or a psychic or puppy in a display window.

"Come look at this, Ray," a woman sitting at the bar would yell across the restaurant and beckon to her husband. "He knows the number of anything. Go on ask him a question."

Come one, come all. Step right up. You can look but don't touch. People did look. People were always looking and pointing and whispering. James's true friends often took turns shooing away spectators.

Often, when James didn't know what to say, he just spit out whatever number was in his head at the time. He had trouble with words. He never knew what type of decorations to hang on his nouns. They came out simple and plain, like stick figures. He thought that there were right and wrong words to answer questions as in the case with numbers. When asked how he felt about something, he always felt like people could tell he was flipping over the drawers in his brain and digging through the rubble, trying to locate the exact statement that correctly described how he felt. He kept everything in his life clean and organized and logical except his feelings and the words that described them. For James, emotions were messy and confusing.

James lit Alison's cigarette for her, partly out of a bartender's habit, partly because it was easier for him to do nice things than say them, but mostly just because he liked to touch her hand. He knew that as he held down the part of the lighter that controlled the flame, she would wrap her hand around his.

There was the soft hum of the lighter and the quiet crunch of cigarette paper burning. Their eyes were on their hands wrapped around one another. Alison took her hand back. He took his lighter back and waited ten seconds before returning it to his pocket.

"You and Sarah won again," he stated, breaking the silence between them.

"We did."

"Strange," he said, looking at the lines on the trunk of a tree across the parking lot.

"What's strange?"

"The odds."

"I told Sarah that Bob might be a psychic."

"Then he would be the one who wins all the time."

"That's true," Alison said, exhaling a line of smoke. "Unless he's just really fucking generous," she added.

James exhaled a line of smoke that crisscrossed and then began dancing in the sunlight with hers. He watched them braid themselves through the air. She threw her cigarette. He threw his cigarette. Then they walked inside together. He reached for Alison's hand, but it was in her pocket. When he noticed this, he pretended to swat a fly.

Even though James had asked Alison, it was Sarah who stayed to work with him through the lull after the lunch rush. The Joes made a portion of coleslaw for both James and Sarah and put them to a blind taste test. Of course, James knew that Big Joe's was in the big bowl and Little Joe's was in the little bowl. Neither Big Joe nor Little Joe could go without taking credit in one way or another.

****

"I love smoking," Alison declared, lighting her first cigarette of the walk on her way home from work with Luke and Trisha.

"We know you do, Ali," Trisha commented. "But you smoke too much."

"Would you rather go without food or cigarettes?" Luke asked Alison.

"For how long?" Alison asked Luke for clarification.

"I don't know, a month."

"I'd rather go without food," Alison answered without hesitation.

"But you'd starve to death!" Trisha exclaimed. Trisha was the type of person who couldn't comprehend going more than twenty minutes without food.

"I would eat the filters," Alison explained and kicked a rock shaped like the state of Texas with the tongue-tied roof of her sneaker.

"What you need is a replacement addiction," Trisha tried.

Luke nodded his head.

"Like sex or something?" Alison asked.

"I don't think chain-fucking is a good idea," Luke said.

"Don't use that word," Trisha scolded Luke and smacked him on the back of his head.

Alison had tried to quit smoking cigarettes only once. It lasted all of six hours, two of which she had bawled like a baby. "I don't need this shit," she had said finally and lit a cigarette.

There are worse habits.

****

As soon as Alison got home, she climbed up on the roof of her house and spread her beach towel on the steaming tar surface. She lay down on her stomach in one of her mom's old swimsuits. It was only slightly too loose for her body. She leafed through an old car magazine and listened to one of her dad's old Springsteen tapes.

Alison had only ever loved two men in her entire life. One was her dad. The other was Bruce Springsteen. And although she had never met Bruce Springsteen and had no idea where her dad was or what he was doing, she felt close to the both of them up there on that roof. She sang along to the music and flipped the pages of her magazine.

"Everything dies, baby; that's a fact." She licked her finger and turned the page. "But maybe everything that dies someday comes back." She licked her finger and turned the page.

"Ali!" Trisha called from the grass down below.

"Sorry, too loud?" Alison turned down the volume and yelled back.

"No, it's fine," Trisha said loudly but slowly. "I was wondering—can you come down for a second and help me? Terrence has put his sister up in the tree," she said in a concerned voice.

"What?" Alison yelled down, leaning over the edge of the roof.

"I'm not kidding! This is the fourth time this month Jennifer is on a branch eight feet up like a gosh dang bluebird!"

Alison shaded her eyes from the sun with her hand and scanned the trees in the yard next to hers. Sure enough, there was a dirty three-year-old sitting on a tree branch, bawling her eyes out.

"I keep trying. But I can't get up to that branch," Luke explained at the top of his tiny lungs. He was standing next to Trisha, holding her nervous hand. Alison could tell that Trisha was squeezing it a bit too hard by both Luke's facial expression and tone of voice.

Terrence was keeled over laughing.

"Don't laugh, Terrence," Trisha scolded. "I am gonna beat your behind once I get your cod jam sister down from there."

"She's not really going to beat you," Luke comforted Terrence.

"The shell I won't!" Trisha yelled, letting go of Luke's hand to smack him on the back of the head again.

"Christ, Trisha. That hurt!"

"Don't use the Lord's name with *me*!"

"She *said* she wanted to be a kitty!" Terrence screamed. He obviously wanted to be a part of the yelling match. Trisha smacked him as well. He stopped laughing to wince at the blow from his mother and rub his head.

Terrence was right, though; for whatever reason, Jennifer did think she was a cat. She crawled on all fours and hissed and meowed all day long. Trisha said the doctor told her it was a phase. So Trisha told everyone that she was just waiting for it to pass. She once told Alison, "It is not such a heavy cross to bear."

Alison turned off the stereo and climbed down from the roof. "Terrence, you can't keep putting your sister up in that tree. She's gonna get hurt," she said to the six-year-old when she got down off of the roof.

"She towd me to do it," Terrence whined and held on to his crotch with both hands.

"You gotta go pee? You better go inside and pee. I am gonna beat you twice as hard if you pee your pants!" Trisha shouted.

Terrence looked at his mother. Her expression was serious. Then he looked to Luke, who was standing strong next to Trisha. Luke's expression mirrored Trisha's.

"Do what your mother says," Luke told Terrence. Terrence immediately turned and ran inside the house.

Alison climbed up the tree to the branch that Jennifer was sitting on. "Come here, you cute little fucker," Alison said, extending an arm toward the toddler. Jennifer scooted on her butt across the branch to the middle of the tree where Alison was. Alison told Jennifer to get on her back and wrap her arms around her neck. As Alison climbed down with Jennifer holding on tightly, Trisha made little noises. For every step and misstep, Trisha let out a tiny squeak.

"Careful. Oh gosh. Golly. Watch yourself. Gosh, golly."

Luke stood silently next to Trisha at the foot of the tree and watched the process without letting a tear escape from his eye. When Alison made it all the way down, toddler unscratched, Trisha threw her arms around both Jennifer and Alison and cried. Luke cried too.

"It's okay," Ali comforted. "Everything is fine."

"Thank you," Trisha said through snot and slobber.

"Thank you," Luke said through slobber and snot.

"You're welcome."

"I'm gonna go yell at my crazy kid," Trisha said, clutching her three-year-old named Jennifer, whose first word was *meow*.

Luke followed Trisha.

****

Trisha was the first person Luke came out of the closet to. She was the least likely to judge and the most likely to forgive or pray. And he wasn't sure which he needed or deserved. Trisha did one better. She not only prayed, but when her prayers didn't work, she tried to save Luke's eternal soul from burning in hell by having sex with him. It was an act not only condoned but also, in her Christlike opinion, blessed by the Lord himself. "You don't know you don't like women if you don't try," was how Luke told his friends she convinced him as they lay naked under a soft pink quilted comforter in her twin canopy bed. But Luke tried. And after the birth of his first and only son, he was still gay. And he was still Trisha's very best friend. Trisha hadn't meant to become pregnant at the age of seventeen. But as she put it, "Maybe Jesus didn't want for you to be a nongay. Maybe he just wanted for the two best friends in the whole dang world to have a beautiful baby boy together."

Luke and Trisha named their child Terrence.

****

Alison's jaw dropped when she opened the refrigerator. She screamed, "Murderrrrrrrrrrrrrrr!" Then she pulled out a package of hot dogs that Sarah or her mother must have bought.

Alison could not handle there being meat in her refrigerator. Whenever Jean or Sarah bought something that was once alive, she knew they tried their best to keep it secret. When they forgot, Alison was flabbergasted, flushed, and hurt. She seized the food, waved it in front of them, and exclaimed, "Our refrigerator is not a cemetery!"

Alison gently picked up the package of hot dogs, pulled open the utensil drawer, grabbed a spoon, and headed back outside. She was still wearing a swimming suit. And as she walked down the stairs that led to her backyard, she pulled a wedgie out of her small bottom with the hand she held the spoon in. "I am sorry you had to see that," she said to the spirit and body of her mother's or sister's ballpark franks. When she got to the bottom of the stairs, she paused and let out a little sigh. *Here comes the hard part*, she thought as she walked toward the back of the yard by a maple tree. She sat on her knees in the dirt and began to dig with the kitchen spoon. The hot dogs waited patiently next to her left ankle. When the hole was deep enough, she carefully placed the hot dogs in it and covered them with dirt. She smoothed out the dirt and said a little prayer.

"I am sorry that you and your friends were murdered and that my mom or my sister was planning to eat you. Please forgive my mom or my sister. I am burying you next to Sarah's turkey sandwich. I think you would have liked that turkey. Say hello to my grandma and grandpa. Amen."

Alison would never admit to the fact that most of the food she had buried in the backyard, including the turkey sandwich she was referring to, did get eaten anyway—by raccoons and opossums and Bob. Jean was never able to figure out why their backyard had become such a happy gathering place for all God's creatures over the past four years even though it was around the time that Alison had read *The Jungle* by Upton Sinclair and become a passionate vegetarian completely overnight. Jean just shook her head and told Alison that all the little animals must really love them. And this made the both of them happy.

When Jean came home from work, Alison was sitting on the couch, watching TV and eating a peanut butter, Tabasco, and jelly sandwich.

"Hi, Alison."

"Hi, yourself," she snapped. "I found an animal in the refrigerator again." She folded her arms tightly against her chest, and her eyes immediately filled with salt water when she looked at her mom.

"Oh, honey, I'm so sorry."

"Mom, you can't keep killing things that are meant to be alive." The tears came as she remembered the wake and funeral she just held in their backyard.

"I *am* sorry," Jean said sympathetically. "It won't happen again, okay? I promise I will talk to Sarah, okay?"

"Okay."

"What did you do today?" She changed the subject.

"I won the lottery and rescued a kid from a tree."

"Oh, I am so proud of you, Boo," Jean said excitedly.

And with Jean's excitement, Alison felt bad for raising her voice toward her mother. Jean was a good mother. Alison knew she lived and breathed for her children. And she knew her mother's only need in the world was to be needed.

"I am glad you're home," Alison said. Then, she added, "What did *you* do today?"

"Well, the girls and I cleaned a bunch of rooms. We had a nice lunch. We cleaned a bunch more rooms. Then I came home to see my beautiful hero daughter." Jean sat down next to Alison on the couch. "What are you watching?"

"*Sister Act 2: Back in the Habit.*"

"Oh, this is such a good movie," Jean said, clapping her hands together.

"I know," Alison said, nodding her head up and down. Jean put her hand on Alison's knee. Alison turned up the volume. She kept her hand there for the entire movie. When it was over, she said, "I will go get groceries so you can have alone time with your date."

"Thanks, Mom. Can you get Doritos?"

"Of course I can, Stan. Have fun!"

CHAPTER 5

———— ✦✦✦✦✦ ————

When a worm is cut in half,
it still wiggles,
only misses its head or tail
a little—
till
it grows back.
Not quite as easy for Alison
to wiggle her way home.
Not quite as easy for her to be alone—
she felt
it hurt
and hurt
until it felt
like rain
covered in blood
and mud
and loss
and shame.

I nstead of returning to the restaurant for the night shift with Trisha and Luke, Alison was given the night off to go on a date.

"What kind of a guy asks a girl out on a Monday?" Doug asked. Then he said, "Oh well, I guess you're not getting any younger."

Alison agreed that she wasn't getting any younger. So when a guy who looked to be about her age scrawled his phone number on his credit card receipt and gave it to her after she had been waiting on him one night, she called him the next day. Alison was the kind of girl who found this sort of thing sweet. "At least he's got a car," Alison defended herself after Sarah yelled at her for not only saving the receipt but for actually calling him.

"At least we've got his credit card number," Sarah responded. Then she added his name to the list she had been keeping on a piece of paper for over six years. On it were names she copied from the credit cards of people she had waited on who were unpleasant, rude, or nontippers. Sarah kept a literal running tab of injustices.

****

Anthony was a shifty-eyed, muscled-up twenty-something-year-old who held on to a football with one hand and rang Alison's doorbell with the other hand. He had dark hair and skin. He was wearing a Nebraska Cornhuskers T-shirt. He looked like he could have been or maybe wanted to be a football player himself. His arm and shoulder muscles were practically begging for a larger-size shirt. And Alison just assumed that it was his equally large leg muscles that made him walk like he was holding a pumpkin between his thighs.

"Come on in," Alison said excitedly.

Anthony came in but only a few steps. Alison went into the kitchen to get a couple of beers. "Don't just stand there!" She laughed as she returned from the kitchen and handed him a beer. She walked over to the sofa, sat down, and then patted a spot on the fabric next to her right knee. "Sit down," she ordered. He walked over to the sofa, set the football on the coffee table, and then cracked open his beer and sat next to Alison.

"So ... what's with the football?" she asked.

"Huh?"

"What's with the football?" she asked again, picking it up off the table and tossing it back and forth in her hands.

"Oh, I don't know, just in case, I guess," he said hurriedly, taking it back.

"O ... kay," she said. *In case of what?* "You said you graduated from the university. Um, what did you study?"

"I said I was done with school," he corrected. "But I didn't graduate ... It got a little tough. My major was football studies," he replied.

Alison looked at him in disbelief. *There is a football studies major? Why? And it's tough? For who?*

"I like cars," Alison said, hoping to create a spark plug of interest.

"Cars are cool," he said, taking a slug of beer.

It was at that moment, just six minutes into the date, that Alison decided the only way this date was going to go well was if she was at the very least mildly intoxicated. And as if Alison needed more persuasion to raise her blood alcohol content, Anthony repeated, "Cars are really cool."

"What do you want to do?" Alison asked.

"I don't know. What do you want to do?" *She knew that was coming.*

"Did you drive or walk?"

"Yeah," he replied.

"Hmmm." She leaned over the arm of the couch to look out the window and see if there was a car in the driveway. There was no car. But there was a massive red pickup truck.

"We could go to the bar by the post office. It has Keno."

"Okay. Is it very far from here?"

Anthony would have been better off not asking this question. Seeing as his brain cells were either busy having a chugging contest or looking at nudie magazines, there was no way for him to understand Alison's answer. Alison never had any idea what the difference was between a block and a foot or a kilometer and a mile. The only way for her to explain how far away something was, was to convert the distance into how many cigarettes you ended up smoking on the way there. Therefore Alison's metric key read something like six blocks equaled one cigarette.

There were two problems with this system. One problem was that a six-cigarette walk and a six-cigarette drive were not quite the same distance. Since Alison rarely drove or rode in a car, she tended to only be able to explain how far away something was to someone who was walking. The second problem was that a nonsmoker really had no idea how long it took to smoke a cigarette or how many blocks one cigarette equated to.

Alison went through the story problem aloud. "Hmmm, let's see … six cigarettes walking. I guess you just divide by two. Three cigarettes away. No, that doesn't sound right. I'm not sure," she said, shaking her head. "How fast do you drive?"

"Huh?" Anthony looked like he had just been hit in the face with a pigskin.

"Never mind."

They took their beers with them in the truck, spilling and gulping over bumps. The two of them were trying to think of things to say but came up with nothing. The football rested on the seat in between them. When they rolled over the gravel parking lot into a parking space, Alison pulled her hair into a low ponytail and hopped down from the truck. Anthony lobbed his half-full beer can at a light pole on the other side of the building. It smacked and exploded against the strong, dark wood. He gave himself two points out loud, grabbed his football, and hopped down from the driver's side. He had already told her, but at this point, Alison had to reconfirm, "You *are* twenty-one, right?"

"Ah," he said sarcastically. "Twenty-four," he added defensively.

"They don't allow footballs in here," Alison said, walking toward him. She took his football and then threw it back into the truck through the driver's side window.

"That sucks," Anthony said not holding the door for her but looking over his shoulder to make sure it did not hit Alison after he walked through it and let go.

****

When Alison and Sarah were in high school, it was customary for the high-schoolers to have parties in the cornfields of the unknowing farmers in nearby towns. The only evidence of anyone having been there after they had gone were the tiny clusters of keg crop circles left over and the butts of cigarettes smashed into the ground. Alison's first sexual encounter took place under the summer stars at one of these types of parties. Alison drank too much and passed out in the dirt. So the majority of this experience took place while she was asleep. Alison was awakened in the middle of a dream. In the dream, she was a whale who was harpooned by a group of men who cheered from a passing boat. The ocean water mixed with her blood. And she felt as if she were drowning. Her insides stung as they began to fill up with a thick saltwater-blood mixture. She smelled the stink of vomit crawling up behind her nose and throat. She could taste everything inside of her coming to the surface. And when she gasped for air, her eyes unlatched themselves and she jolted upright. She saw what looked like one of the fishermen cramming himself inside her, and she screamed. This surprised and scared a very eager teenage boy half to death. He hopped off of her so quickly that her eyes were unable to adjust to being open. He ran into the dark. His friends who had gathered in a circle around the two of them dropped their cigarettes and keg cups. They ran too. Alison threw up all over her right rib cage. Those who were in other parts of the field came to find the girl to whom the scream belonged.

It took Sarah and James at least five minutes to find her because many of the headlights they had relied on to guide them through the field were pulling away and facing the road. Alison was gagging and convulsing when they found her. She told James and Sarah but no one else what had happened. Long after they left the pesticides and thick cornstalks, the boys returned for their kegs. But James and Sarah rolled all six of them behind a barn and came back to drink from them for several weeks. That was the only revenge Sarah's sister ever got. And it was more for Sarah than for Alison. Because when Sarah told her about it, Alison said that it was unnecessary and slightly cruel. "So it is cruelty not beauty that is in the eye of the beholder," Sarah told her. But Alison knew both Sarah and James spent years conducting an investigation, relentlessly asking questions of anyone who would listen so that they could pursue a more fitting revenge in which they took turns smashing that guy's balls with a baseball bat. They never found out who it was. Sarah never got her revenge on the boy who raped her little sister.

"Good," Alison told Sarah. "I would never forgive myself if you hurt someone because of me." But she knew saying that only made Sarah want to smash his balls more.

Alison's first sexual encounter didn't turn her away from sex. It had quite the opposite effect. And when Alison's father left, she began having sex with anyone she could, each time trying to make it feel better than the last. She fell in love with sex every time she had it. She thought sex was love. To her, it had never been proven otherwise. She hurriedly jumped into it, couldn't wait for it to happen. And happen it did, over and over again. It happened so much that it began to feel like making a free throw or smoking weed or knowing the answer to the daily double on *Jeopardy* ... only mildly rewarding. But she kept trying, kept looking in the only place she had ever thought to look.

****

It was strange not to have Alison at the restaurant, as if a piece of the machine were missing. The waitstaff was slightly behind their regular pace. And the table that gave Sarah a baby to hold while they got settled into their seats did not speed things up. Sarah scanned the restaurant for someone, anyone, to help her. She had her tray between her legs and her notebook under her arm. It was about to slip. She would have rather dropped the kid. He or she stank and was about to start crying. Sarah kept a smile on her face. But it felt uncomfortable, as if it had been tricked into sitting there the way that she had been tricked into holding that squirming bag of poop.

"Okay, I'll take her now," the mother said, reaching out to take her child back. "Thank you."

"No. Thank you," Sarah said. "I just love children." The baby giggled. "That *was* funny, wasn't it?" she whispered to the baby before she handed her back.

But what was really funny was that flashing neon sign Doug put up on the side of the restaurant that faced the interstate. At night, it grabbed the attention of every passing trucker and pulled them inside. The sign repeated, "Food … Beer … Food … Beer," over and over again in alternating colors. On it, there was the silhouette of a big-busted lady holding a tray. No one knew why Doug put that lady on there. But you could imagine what most guys thought when they clicked on their blinker and pulled off the interstate for it. And you could also imagine their surprise when they came in, sat down at a table, and a little gay cowboy asked if he could start them off with an iced tea.

"Ain't there no dancers in here?" a guy with a beard that had cigarette ashes in it asked angrily.

"No, sir," Luke said.

"This a queer bar?" another guy with tattoos instead of sleeves took a toothpick out of his mouth to ask.

"No, sir."

"Well, bring us a pitcher then," the guy with the beard said.

"Of iced tea?" Luke asked, smiling.

"Hell no, boy! Of beer! And tell that lady with the tits to bring it to us," the guy with tattoos said and pointed toward Sarah.

"A pitcher with tits, coming right up," Luke said, laughing as he walked toward Sarah. She was ringing in an order at the register, which was not far from Luke's table. She immediately shook her head no before he could ask if she would wait on the table.

"I just held a baby. I am not waiting on those toolboxes too," she said.

"Please," he whined. "They're gonna tit you better than me."

"Did you say 'tit'?"

"No, I said 'tip,'" Luke lied.

"Fine, but you owe me, even if I do get a good tip."

"Thank you. Thank you."

"Which I won't," she added as she rang in a pitcher of beer. When she brought them their pitcher, she said, "My name's Sarah. So if you need anything, just call."

The two men were not looking at her face. Not even close.

"Can we get your phone number, then?" the guy with the toothpick in his mouth said, finally looking up from her boobs.

Sarah rolled her eyes. Then she shook her head. "No. Just call *my name*. I'll hear you," she said, setting down their glasses and pitcher of beer.

When Sarah walked into the kitchen, Big Joe and Little Joe were at it again. This time, they were having a spelling bee using only perishable vocabulary.

"Casserole," James said, taking his plates from the window and putting them on a tray.

"You give him casserole?" Little Joe shouted. "You give me *French words* ... and he gets *casserole*!"

"Lychees are from China," James corrected.

"I bet you nobody in China's ever heard of a damn lychee. They probably heard *casserole* a couple hundred times. But they ain't never heard of a lychee! I'm not spelling if this is how you're going to play!"

Big Joe pushed Little Joe out of the way and declared, "I've heard of a lychee!"

"No, you haven't," Little Joe said, walking toward the fryer.

"Yes, I have," Big Joe said defiantly.

"Bullshit!" Little Joe yelled.

"Sorry to interrupt, guys, but how long on my burgers?" Sarah asked, sticking her head through the food window.

"Oh, it's going to be a while," Little Joe said. "I gotta go to China to get some lychees to put on top."

"Actually, you don't have to go all the way to China," James began.

Sarah could see Little Joe's nostrils flaring. And before James could finish, he was hit in the stomach with an onion.

"They asked me to pick the words," James told Sarah as he picked up a tray and put it on his shoulder. Then he added, "I thought everybody knew what lychees were." On his way out, James was hit in the back with a carrot. Big Joe stuck his enormous face through the window and motioned for Sarah to come closer.

"I have no idea what a lychee is," he whispered, smiling.

Little Joe shoved him out of the way and flung Sarah's burgers into the food window.

"Spell *baby* why don't you?" Sarah told Little Joe as she grabbed her burgers and sprinted toward the door before there was time enough for him to hit her with a nearby fruit or vegetable. On her way out of the kitchen, she told Trisha not to go in there for a while. "Let it cool down," Sarah said.

She was not the slightest bit surprised when Trisha answered, "But it's a *kitchen*; isn't it supposed to be hot in there?"

CHAPTER 6

Linda made a cake
in an un-air-conditioned kitchen
that dates back to the seventies.
Grease-stained appliances and
a stove that won't shine
even after a Brillo pad
and what's left of the half water, half 409.

She stuck it in the oven for two and a half hours
and decorated it all by herself
with tiny frosted flowers,
put it on the fancy plate—
the one they only use for parties,
the one that looks like real crystal,
with a star that sparkles in the middle.

She wished he had called
to say
he'd stopped at the bar
after work
again,
that she should go ahead
and blow out the candles.

She wished her kitchen were new
and that she didn't have to wait
for him
to make enough money
to buy clothes to make money in
or for her to bear enough children
to bear the state she's in
the middle of America
and at the end of her rope—
maybe she'll hang on,
maybe she'll let go
of all these dreams.
They really are such little things.

L inda knocked on Jean's door, holding a box of wine and a jigsaw puzzle. Jean smiled and took the box of wine from her. Linda smiled back and followed her friend into the kitchen. Jean set the box on the counter and paused to look disapprovingly at a piece of paint peeling its way down the kitchen wall. Underneath it was the head of a flower. "Don't look at me," she said, narrowing her eyes at the flower's little blue face. "I didn't paint over you. That was done before I moved in." She licked her hand and then touched the backing of the paint with her spit. "See ya later, alligator," she said as she placed it back on top of the wallpaper peeking out from behind.

"I like your kitchen," Linda said softly as she dumped the puzzle onto the table. "I always wanted pretty tile like you have."

"The paint is peeling," Jean said, taking plastic cups out of a cupboard. She poured wine into them and handed one to Linda.

"But you have a new refrigerator and lots of plants," Linda said, taking a sip and then sitting down in front of the puzzle.

"None of our plates match," Jean said, sitting down next to Linda.

"We eat off of paper most of the time," Linda said as she began flipping over the puzzle pieces.

Jean did the same. "Linda, these pieces are all different sizes. You have like three different puzzles in this box!"

"I do?" She picked up several pieces and examined them. "Huh, I guess I do."

"Come on; we don't have husbands anymore," Jean said, picking up her cup of wine. "Let's get out of the kitchen," she added as she grabbed a bag of potato chips from the counter and Linda's hand at the same time. She gently pulled her up from her chair and led her out onto the porch. Linda tried to think but couldn't remember if her husband had ever helped her up from a chair. The gesture made her sad and grateful at the same time.

It was the kind of summer night when Linda had to shake the mosquitoes loose from the folds of her shirt and smack their blood-filled bellies open on the surface of her skin. But it didn't bother Linda. She had Jean. And Jean had half an ounce of illegal substances. The radio was pressed against the window screen so that they could listen to music together. They listened to the same program every night with love songs and dedications. People called in and told their stories, and the DJ, she found a song, the perfect song, for the caller every time.

Jean and Linda both had their legs up on the porch railing and were taking turns pulling hot green wax off of them with long, thick pieces of tape. They took turns pulling and screaming. When they were finished and their legs were peeled raw, Jean lit a joint and passed it to Linda.

"Oh snap," Jean said, snapping her fingers together.

"What?" Linda asked.

"Oh snap," Jean repeated, snapping her fingers again. "I heard it on TV, I think. Or maybe I heard it from Trisha's husband. I can't even remember now."

"What's it mean?"

"I think it means pay attention. Like when someone is snapping a picture."

"That's cute, Jean," she said and smiled. "You mind if I use that?"

"Go right ahead, Fred."

"My legs really hurt. Why didn't you light this thing before? Isn't marijuana a painkiller or something?"

"I have no idea. Sorry!" Jean giggled. "Boo Boo said this wasn't supposed to hurt as much. It *did* hurt less than the last time. Don't you think?"

"I don't know. Maybe. Maybe Boo Boo is just used to it. She's got a much higher tolerance for pain than we do."

There was a caller on the line who was choking down tears and talking about having her only son going off to college. Afterward, the DJ played something by Tracy Chapman. Jean and Linda cried through the entire song. When the song was over, Linda looked at Jean and said, "I am so glad I've got you to cry with."

"I have no idea why we listen to this show."

"Everyone listens to this show," Linda assured Jean as she blew snot into a ball of tape covered in hairy wax.

Jean took bite of a potato chip and said, "Our kids sure are growing up."

"You raised them girls real well. It's so hard to do it by yourself," Linda said.

"You raised those boys well too. And you never had any help."

There was a silence between them that lasted several minutes and was filled with thought. Linda and Jean were forced to help one another, like seeds that were planted too close together. Jean took Linda's hand. Linda looked up at her.

"You helped me a lot. Not just with my boys," Linda said.

Jean nodded and let another tear escape from the corner of her left eye.

"I hope our kids are never lonely," Linda said suddenly.

"They'll never be lonely. They've got each other."

"And we have each other too," Jean said, squeezing Linda's hand. Both their hands were salted and oily from the potato chips and hot and sticky from the humidity and wax. But they tightened around one another anyway.

"You know what I think?" Linda said, looking out into the trees for the right words. "I think you changed my life around." She looked at Jean appreciatively.

"You helped me too," Jean said, squeezing Linda's hand again.

"I'm sorry I wasn't there like I should have been when your husband left. It was only a few weeks after my Charles passed."

"I know that, Linda. You don't have to be sorry. You have always been there when I needed you." She took a sip from her wine and added, "If you don't have a husband, you damn well better have a girlfriend."

"Yeah, but I always wanted both," Linda said, looking out at the trees again. "Do you think we would be this close if our husbands were still here?"

"I don't know. That's kind of a sad question," Jean said.

"Sometimes the truth is sad," Linda said, looking up at Jean. "You know it feels so strange to be single at the age of forty-five."

"We're not single. We have each other ... and we have our children."

"You know what I mean. Having no one to tell you that you are beautiful when you are not. Having no one to brush your hair off of your face," Linda explained with slightly salty eyes.

"You *are* beautiful," Jean said. "And I will get your hair when it's in your face. You just let me know."

There was a fresh breeze that tickled the leaves on the branches so that, only for a few seconds, it appeared that the maple trees were waving at Linda and her best friend.

****

After Trisha left for the night and the only customers still in the restaurant were the ones drinking at the bar, Luke and Sarah pulled two sticky, wobbly stools closer to one another and waited at the bar for James to make them a couple of drinks.

"Well, how much have you got?" Luke asked, looking from his pile of credit card slips to Sarah's and then back to his like they were two kids who had just dumped trick or treats from a couple of yellowed pillowcases and were about to start trading Snickers and Kit-Kats.

"Doug sure didn't stay for very long today," Sarah said as she counted her tips.

"Yeah, fifty-three minutes," James confirmed. "Hope he's okay."

"I don't," Sarah added. "I hope he's got diarrhea." Then Sarah told Luke how much money she had made. "Forty-three, ninety-six."

"Fifty-six, even. Guess I buy then, huh."

"Even when you win, you lose," Sarah said.

"What's a drink for losers, then?"

"Losers take shots, I think," Sarah answered with a smile.

"You're right." He smiled back.

"I'll pick," James said, reaching over the bar and grabbing their cash-outs. He took off his watch and put the dollar bills into neat piles. He straightened them. Then he restraightened them. Then he washed his hands because it was a quarter after eleven. After he dried them off with a towel and placed the towel back on the towel rack, he grabbed two shot glasses and set them in front of Luke and Sarah.

"Best bang for your buck," Sarah told James who was already pouring shots of whiskey into the shot glasses.

"Doug's not here, so I don't want your bucks. But I will give him a bang for his buck."

"To Doug's bucks," Sarah said, lifting her shot glass.

"That deserves a round of applause! Where are Doug's corduroys when you need them?" Luke asked, swallowing the whiskey.

Then all three of them scanned the bar to make sure none of Doug's friends were sitting at it. There was one. But he laughed too, even though there was no way he knew how funny it really was.

"I wish Alison were here," James said.

"You know if you want her to love you back, all you have to do is find her dad," Luke said, not looking directly at James.

"Unless you find him with his new girlfriend or family and he's a big piece of shit. Then you will destroy her."

"What makes you think I'm in love with Alison?" James asked, looking at Luke. "And your dad isn't a piece of shit. He was more of a dad to me than my own dad was," he added, shifting his gaze toward Sarah.

"You look at her the way Trisha looks at chocolate cake," Sarah answered for Luke. "And be my guest, James. 'Cause I've tried and I don't know how to fix Ali," Sarah said. "She's only happy on the outside. And to be perfectly honest, she's about one misadventure away from a meltdown."

****

James's father, Charles Bradley Bluff, was a mean man who had rotted from the inside out. Linda once told James that before the booze broke him, his father was kind and reliable. But as far back as James could remember, his father cursed and spit the shells of sunflower seeds all over the yard. When he opened his mouth, his breath smelled like the corpses of dead birds mixed with the soup that boils in a septic tank. His yellow skin leaked sweat and whiskey through its pores. His body was stained with grease and tattoos. His lips were folded into a permanent smirk, as if he thought your existence funny. He was always making jokes. James's dad made the kind of jokes that were either cruel or offensive. The more he hurt or offended, the funnier he thought himself. He was always shoving or pushing things out of his way. James said it was because Charles Bradley Bluff thought the world owed him a clear path through it. Instead of affection, James's father showed something similar to disgust at the sight of his family. And when Luke arrived one summer day to become a part of it, Charles Bradley Bluff surveyed the weakest-looking little boy he had ever seen in his life and said to Luke, "The only thing worse than a weakling is a colored one."

Alison said if God had given James's dad a heart that he must have put it in backward or upside down. Luke said it was best to just apologize upon seeing the man. James said he wasn't going to let himself ever end up like his father. Sarah said that man's existence was proof that life was cruel and unfair.

****

There was a man at the other end of the bar who seemed to be watching Sarah, Luke, and James. James walked over to him. "I haven't seen you in here before. You live in town?"

"No, just visiting a friend."

"You seem to paying an awful lot of attention to our conversation."

The man rubbed the beard on his chin for a few seconds and took a swig of beer. "I was just thinking I may know someone who can help you find whoever it is you are looking for. You got a pen?"

James grabbed a pen from a cup next to the cash register and handed it to him. The man picked up a napkin, wrote something down on it, and handed it back to James. "Tell him Fish sent you."

"Fish?" Luke asked.

"Yeah, like tuna. It's a nickname," he answered. "This guy owes me a favor," he said, pointing at the napkin he had just given James. "Sounds like you guys need one," he said, eyeing Sarah. He looked at James and added, "Hope it helps you get the girl." Then he finished the rest of his beer and got up from the bar stool. "Good night," he said and walked out the door.

"Well, that was weird as hell," Luke said, looking at the empty bar stool.

"What's it say?" Sarah asked, snatching the napkin from James's hand. "Holy shit!" Her eyes widened.

"What?" Luke almost screamed. "What's it say?"

She held the napkin in front of his face. It read, "Anthony Milano 1-306-843-9991."

"This is the guy Alison went on a date with."

"Are you sure?" Luke asked.

Sarah jumped off of her bar stool, pulled the paper from her apron, and found where she had scribbled Anthony's name and credit card number. She showed it to Luke. James grabbed it to see for himself. He shook his head and ran a hand through his hair.

"What the hell is going on?" he said, looking at Sarah.

"I'll call home," Sarah said, going behind the bar and picking up the phone.

James and Luke were stone still while Sarah stood with the phone to her ear. She shook her head. "No answer."

"Okay. Luke and I will go out looking for her," James told her. "We're closed. Go home, everyone!" he yelled to the three people still left in the bar. "You better go home and wait for her," he told Sarah. "We will call each other if we find her. Deal?"

"I should go with you."

"Alison is going to go home; she may already be on her way. You need to be there."

"But I—"

"What if she shows up with him?"

"You're right. I should be there."

****

When Sarah got home, the house was dark except for one lonely light bulb hanging on to a whirring ceiling fan. Jean was asleep, and Alison was still out. The only trace of Alison ever being there were the rings from the beers she drank with Anthony left to dry out and stain the wood on the coffee table. Alison should have been home from her date already. *Who the fuck is this guy? Is she safe? Did she sleep with him? Of course she did. She sleeps with every first date. If Dad were still here, she wouldn't have to sleep around to fill up the giant void in her heart.*

"Fuck you, Dad," Sarah whispered into the air.

She grabbed the cordless phone, sat down on the couch, and stared at it. The last bulb inside the light fixture was flickering like a strobe light, as if it were hanging on to its last florescent watt until Alison came home. Sarah began biting her nails. *Everything is fine.* Sarah turned on the television to calm her mind. And the light did, in fact, give itself up. Alison would have called if she was not coming home. She would have called either way. The television was playing a rerun of *The Cosby Show*. Cliff was hiding his hoagie sandwich under the couch cushions. *Alison is fine*, Sarah told herself over and over again until she finally fell asleep, sitting up on the couch, still holding the phone. Sarah's dream had both Alison and the Cosby family in it. But her dad must have known better than to show his face in her sleep.

****

As it turned out, Anthony did know quite a bit about cars. While they talked about the only subject they had in common, Alison got very drunk. She realized this when she had trouble saying "pliers." As Anthony leaned in closer, Alison not only smelled but felt his tequila-and-lime breath. The smoke from Alison's cigarette wrapped itself around her and her date. And they kissed. It was not the kiss of a Porsche touching someone else's fender softly while parallel parking. But then again, how many Porsches don't just get a valet? It was the lusty, commonplace kiss of jumper cables charging a juiceless battery in the winter. The red warning light went on. They paid their bill and slipped outside to look under Anthony's hood. No grease. No dust. His wires were strong and secure. Alison was impressed.

"Most people don't take as good of care on the inside as on the outside."

"Do you want to see the inside?" Anthony asked.

They got into the truck and drove a couple of miles down the road. He put on the parking brake. The kissing that occurred was minimal and rough. Anthony pushed Alison's tongue down with his tongue so hard that it weighed on her lower jaw. Then he pulled his tongue back as quickly as he extended it. He sucked on her tongue as if it were a cigarette about to go out. He sucked until she pulled her face away from his. He pushed her into the seat of the truck, which was sticky and smelled like a McDonald's value meal. He undressed Alison for all the stars to see. She looked up through the sunroof at them as she slid down and Anthony climbed on top, jamming his super unleaded gasoline pump into her fuel tank, filling it up and over. She wrapped her arms around him. But he pulled away. He elbowed her in the face. Then he opened up the passenger-side door and kicked her out with his left size 13. He pulled his pants up and drove away before Alison was able to pick herself up from the jewels of a litter-filled ditch. It began to rain from what seemed like no clouds at all. It rained down on Alison, who just sat there by the side of the road, wondering what to do. It almost felt good. *That time, I got really close to good*, she thought. But even objects in the mirror are closer than they seem. Alison looked through the rain into the stars. She thought she saw Orion put down what looked like his arrow but may have been his foot. Alison weakly rose from her knees, brushed off the dirt and rocks, and began to walk home.

****

"I'll get it!" Sarah shouted from the middle of her dream when she heard the front door open. She used the light from the TV to make her way toward the front door, which was still open. She looked around but didn't see Alison.

"Alison?" she said softly over the lump in her throat. Sarah knew before she even touched or heard or saw Alison that something was wrong.

"I'm here," a small voice called from the floor.

Sarah looked down. Alison was sitting with her back against the wall, her knees to her chest. She smelled of salt, sweat, dirt, and sex.

Sarah fell to the floor and wrapped her arms around her sister. Alison sobbed into Sarah's hair as Sarah held her tightly.

"I'm here, Ali. It's okay. I'm here."

Alison clung to Sarah like a frightened child, awkwardly digging her nails into Sarah's shoulder blades. She used the flashlight of the moon shining in through the front door and the glow of the TV from across the room to examine Alison's physical condition. She surveyed her body first, scrapes and dirt. Then she gently pulled Alison's head from her shoulder and looked at her face. Alison closed her eyes. More scrapes and dirt.

"What happened?" Sarah begged.

Alison put her head back on Sarah's shoulder. Sarah held her for several minutes without turning on a light or shutting the door, without doing anything but rubbing her back. Suddenly, Alison loosened her grip, slapped her legs together, and threw them at the door, slamming it shut. Then she came clamoring back up into Sarah's arms.

"Where is he?" Sarah probed softly.

"He left me by the road," Alison whispered in Sarah's ear.

Sarah could feel Alison's breath slowing down. But she was still clinging, like a cat you try to put into a bathtub.

"Don't tell anyone. He just kicked open the car door and threw me out."

Sarah held her loosely. She didn't know where her sister was hurt. Sarah knew Ali wasn't, but for some reason, she couldn't stop thinking, *My sister is just a baby.*

The synapses in Sarah's brain fired and misfired. The sparks suddenly struck anger. Sarah pictured this guy with thick, coarse whiskers that scratch like wool and jutting veins, pulsating all the way down to his groin. She pictured him reaching over Alison's back for the handle on the car door and flinging her in only a T-shirt and her pants around her ankles from his semen-stained backseat onto some gravel road. Sarah's skin grew tight over stiffening joints and muscles. She felt her blood getting thick and heavy.

"Let's just forget about it." Alison's voice wavered.

"No, Alison." Sarah's voice was calm but louder. "You can't just forget all the terrible things that happen to you. You just can't."

"Shhhhh. Don't wake Mom." Alison's voice matched Sarah's in tone but not volume.

"I'm calling the cops."

"Sarah, what are they going to do?" Alison asked. "They can't even help us figure out what happened to Dad. How are they going to find a dumb jock?" She was still tightly hanging on to Sarah.

"You're bleeding, aren't you?"

Alison lifted her head. Sarah's eyes had adjusted, and she could see Alison's face. It was dirty except for the tiny tear highways. Her bare legs were scraped, jigger-bug bitten, and mud-ridden. Her knees were puffy like a spider had gotten in and laid a sack of eggs just beneath the skin.

"I told you he threw me out of the car. We had sex, and he threw me out of the car," she blurted. "It's not a fucking crime."

"Why are your knees bleeding?" Sarah accused without meaning to.

"I landed on them when he threw me out of the car." She had stopped crying.

Sarah didn't want to scold her. She didn't deserve it. She couldn't lecture her on her promiscuity or for putting herself in these places. Sarah had always admired Alison's ability to do whatever she wanted whenever she felt like doing it. She had to assume that this was her sister's way of coping, filling herself up with as many men as she could to make up for the one good one she had lost—everyone had lost. Sarah knew what everyone thought about her sister. She had heard them say Alison slept with more men than you could count, didn't wear underwear, and used the f-word incessantly. But using the f-word was not a crime. And neither was needing or leaving or grieving or believing. The only crime was not knowing when you should. Alison did what she felt and said what she meant. And to Sarah that was what made Alison beautiful.

"We will talk about it in the morning," she said, helping Alison up from the floor. She walked with her to her bedroom. And after she had helped her into her bed, she lay there until Alison fell asleep. Alison sobbed softly until she drifted into sleep. When Sarah heard her begin to snore, she got up from her bed to call James and Luke. She kissed her on the forehead and then tucked the sheets tightly around her small frame. "No monsters are getting into your dreams," she whispered.

****

James answered the phone on the second ring. "Is she okay? What happened? We almost came over. Did she tell you about the guy?"

"She's home. I didn't talk to her about Anthony. She needs rest."

"What do you mean you didn't talk to her about him?"

"James, it would have been too much for her. We can talk to her tomorrow. She is our priority, not this guy."

"She's okay then?"

"She will be. Go to sleep, and I'll call you in the morning."

"Promise?"

"If I don't … you know where I live."

Two Cherries

CHAPTER 7

It was 8:03
in the morning.
Alison first struck anger
like a nerve,
wanting more than anything
not to deserve
him leaving
her
to go back
to the way things were
before things weren't
the same
every day,
waiting for his dramatic
return
return
return—
in between
each day
and each dream
his memory
stitched into
each hole,
rip, and seam
very slowly unraveling.

lison awoke to the roar and squeal of a garbage truck in front of her house. As she turned her head to see out the window, she felt a sharp pain in her neck that didn't end until it hit her tailbone. She lay still and watched the garbage men pick up and turn over each shiny metal can. The past seven days of her family's life were dumped out and smashed down. A smell of rotten bananas, molded pizza crusts, and eggs came in through the window screen along with the noise of the truck and the laughter of the two men in garbage-covered jumpsuits, joking with one another. She winced as she pulled down her covers. Her knees were raw, and her sheets had little rocks in them. She got out of bed, went to her dad's picture on the desk, and picked it up.

"Good morning, Dad," she said, looking at his face. Then she threw the picture at the window so hard that both garbage men turned to look. "It's not fucking funny!" she yelled at them. Then she tore her comforter and sheets off the bed and threw them. Then she took her arm to her desk and swiped everything on it onto the floor. Everything crashed down into a pile on the blue carpet. "And you!" she turned and screamed at the cat in the swimsuit on the calendar, "You think your swimsuit is so fucking cute!" She grabbed a pencil from the floor and threw it at the cat. Then she grabbed a half-eaten apple and threw it. Her camera. A book. A candle. A plant. She kept going until Sarah came running into the room.

"Ali, what the hell is going on!" Sarah shouted. She looked at the broken picture and the papers and clutter all over Alison's floor.

"What do you mean? I'm fucking redecorating. See? Doesn't that broken picture of Dad spruce up the place?" she said, pointing to their dad's cracked face. "And the plant wasn't getting enough light, so I just dumped his ass on the floor," she said, nodding toward a pile of dirt, leaves, and broken clay. "You can see the sun now. Can't you, you stupid fucking plant?" she yelled at the pile of dirt.

"Um." Sarah just stood there and stared at Alison. "I think this is the first time I've ever seen you mad," Sarah said cautiously. "I'm not really sure what to do."

"Oh, you can do nothing. How about that? I will make posters and put them on every fucking wall in town and send them all over every other town and get in trouble for using Doug's copy machine every other week, and you just go ahead and do nothing!"

Jean appeared in the doorway, fresh from the shower. "What is all the screaming ..." She stopped when she saw Alison's face. Alison had no idea what her face looked like, but she could feel her right eye was puffy and her cheek was embedded with small pieces of gravel.

"I fell. It's no big deal. I'm fine," she said, breathing hard.

"The heck you are. You look like someone threw a porcupine at your face!"

"She's fine," Sarah interjected.

Alison was grateful that she did. Alison didn't want to tell her mom what had happened to her. She already had enough emotions pulsing through her. She didn't want to add the one that would come from the pain she saw on her mother's face when she reminded her how big of a whore her youngest daughter was. But she would if pressed. Lying sat about as well as food poisoning in Alison's stomach. It wanted back out of her body so badly that it would make her sick.

"She fell in the driveway last night. She tripped over the basketball," Sarah said.

"I didn't leave the porch light on, did I? God, Alison. I am so sorry. I could have sworn I left it on. What is the matter with me? One of you girls is going to get eaten by raccoons or something one of these days ... if I can't remember to keep that light on. I am so sorry. Wait! What happened to your floor?"

"It's okay, Mom. Seriously. I went to bed when it was dark. I ran into the desk. I'm fine."

Jean shook her head back and forth, back and forth, as if she were trying to get rid of the image of ravenous raccoons tearing Alison's limbs apart or Alison running into her desk so hard that every single thing on it fell into a pile on the floor.

"Let me get the Neosporin," Jean said, already on her way into the bathroom.

Alison looked at Sarah. "Thanks," she said.

"Oh, it's the least I can do now!" Jean called from one of the bathroom cabinets. "I already left it pitch-black for you out there to trip and fall and hit your poor face on Lord knows what." Jean was mumbling something about a tetanus shot to herself as she came back into the bedroom with the Neosporin. Alison sat cross-legged in the middle of her broken room and heart as her mom rubbed Neosporin into the cuts on her cheek.

"Now I am just going to get a piece of meat from the freezer, and I want you to hold it on your eye for a while."

"A piece of *what*?"

"Peas," Jean struggled. "A piece of peas … I mean a bag of peas. Frozen ones. In a bag."

Alison could not take it anymore. She was just about to punch something when she heard the honk from Boo Boo's sedan in the driveway.

"Oh that's my ride!" Jean exclaimed. She ran out of the bedroom and reappeared a few seconds later with a bag of frozen peas. She handed them to Alison. "Are you going to be okay?" she asked, leaning down and looking into Alison's eyes.

"Yes," Alison lied harder than she had ever lied to anyone.

No sooner than two minutes after Jean left for work, there was a knock at the door.

"Who the fuck is that?" Alison snapped at Sarah as she stood up.

"We're coming in," Luke called from the front door.

"Um, just a minute! We're getting dressed!" Sarah yelled.

"No, we're not. I just finished tearing my room apart, and Sarah doesn't want you to see so come on back!" Alison yelled.

Luke and James stood in Alison's doorway, staring.

"I'm redecorating," she said in a loud voice.

"What happened to your face?" James asked.

Alison touched her face, slowly feeling the scabs and rocks. She tried to imagine what she must look like. Her body relaxed suddenly without warning, and she weakly sat back down on the bed. James came to sit next to her and touched her hand.

"Are you okay?" Luke asked, not moving from the doorway.

"Nope." She shook her head. "I'm a fucking mess," she said softly.

"So Sarah told you about the guy at the bar?" Luke asked.

"She doesn't need to hear about it right now," Sarah scolded Luke.

"Hear about what? What guy at the bar?" Alison saw Luke look to Sarah to see if he should continue talking or stop.

Sarah shook her head no.

"What guy at the bar, Luke?"

"Excuse me just one second. I have to run to the bathroom," Luke said and quickly left.

"What guy at the bar, James?" Alison asked, turning to face James.

"What happened to your face?" he asked again.

"I went on a date. The guy elbowed me and threw me out of the fucking truck after—"

"She fell," Sarah interrupted.

"After we had sex," Alison finished her sentence. "Everyone knows I have sex with anyone who wants to. It's not a fucking secret, Sarah," she said, glaring at her sister. She turned back toward James. "Now what about the guy at the bar?" she shouted.

James looked at her and calmly told her, "There was a guy at Doug's last night said he might know someone who can help us find your dad. He gave us this," he said, pulling the napkin with Anthony's name on it from his pocket and handing it to her. She tilted her head and looked at it for a few seconds.

"Is this a fucking joke? Why does everyone think everything is so fucking funny today? ... First the garbage men, then the fucking cat in her swimsuit ..."

"It's real, Ali," Sarah said.

Luke was back to standing in the doorway again. Alison looked up at him. He nodded his head yes. She looked back down at the napkin.

"Wait a second. That's not his number," she said, getting up and opening a desk drawer. She pulled Anthony's credit card receipt from the drawer, the one he had written his number on. "See," she said, bringing the paper to Sarah and showing her both the napkin and the credit card receipt.

"Maybe he has two phones," Sarah replied.

"Maybe it's a totally different person with the same name," Luke added.

"Call it," Alison said, handing James back the napkin.

Luke ran to get the phone. When he returned, he gave the phone to James, who looked at Alison.

She nodded. "Do it," she said. "And put it on fucking speaker."

James turned the speaker on and began dialing.

"Hello?" the voice on the other end answered. Everyone looked at Alison. She grabbed a pen and paper off of the floor and wrote, "Not the same guy." Then she held it in front of her body without a smile, like someone was about to take her mug shot. Everyone was quiet.

"Hello?" the voice said again, loudly.

"Hi. May I speak with Anthony Milano?" Sarah asked.

"Who the fuck is this?"

"My name is Sarah. I was calling to see if you might be able to help me find someone."

"Isn't that the police's job?" he asked.

"Sure, if you like waiting," Alison blurted.

He chuckled. "I'm sorry; I don't do that anymore," he said.

"Fish said you might be able to help us," Sarah added.

"Of course he did. That bastard. All right. There's a coffee shop in Wilmonte. I'll be there around ten fifteen. Bring a picture and as much information as you can on the target—Social Security number, license plate, that kind of stuff."

"The target?" Alison asked, scrunching up her face.

"The person you are looking for," he clarified.

"We don't want you to kill him," Luke jumped in.

"We just want you to help us find out where he is," Sarah added.

He chuckled. "Fuckin' Fish …" He paused for a moment. "Well, all right. I'll see you later."

"Okay, see you."

Alison pressed end on the phone still held loosely in James's hands.

"Did we just call a hit man?" Luke asked, biting on his lower lip.

"Sure sounds like it," James said.

"Who is this fucking Fish guy anyway? I mean, did he seem like the kind of guy who kills people and then cuts them up?" Alison asked.

Luke shook his head no. "He seemed normal."

"He was nice," James added.

"Well, guess it pays to know Fish," Alison said as she stood up.

"So you're going?" Luke asked skeptically.

"Of course we're fucking going!" Alison exclaimed, looking at Sarah.

"Okay, we are going. But we're bringing Big Joe," Sarah told her.

"Deal," Alison said, grabbing Sarah's hand and shaking it.

"I gotta get to Trisha's for breakfast," Luke said. "Ali, you be careful. And, Sarah ..." He paused and said, "You don't be a bitch." Then he laughed and ran out of the room.

****

"Morning!" Trisha yelled, walking into the kitchen where her parents were having oatmeal for breakfast and playing hearts. They were stuck. As usual, someone had forgotten whose turn it was and they were arguing back and forth. Trisha had a kid on each hip.

"It's my trump," Trisha's mom said, sipping her tea.

"No, no," her dad said, putting his wrinkled hand over the pile and sliding it toward himself. His wedding ring clicked on the tabletop. "It's my trump, ya old bag."

"Hey, Mom, Dad ... Good morning," Trisha repeated, setting Terrance down. Jennifer wiggled. Trisha set her down too.

"Whose trump?" Trisha's dad asked her.

"What?" Trisha asked, turning her good ear toward her father and cupping her hand around it.

"Whose trump?" Trisha's dad asked louder.

"Mom's," Trisha said defiantly. Whenever she was asked this question, Trisha simply allotted the trump to the person who didn't ask. It was a system of fairness. And according to Trisha, the world was fair. It was also a system that neither of her parents had been able to figure out since she started using it.

"Haha, my trump, Frankenstein!" Trisha's mom said, taking the pile and pulling it toward herself.

"It's always been the women against the men around here," Trisha's dad grumbled, putting his fist under his chin and resting on it. "First, you want my trump; then you want my money. What's next? You want my wiener too?"

"Oh please, Henry. No one wants that old thing!" Trisha's mom yelled, slapping her hands on her knees.

"Last night, you wanted it, Pam ... Couldn't get enough of it, as a matter of fact!" he shouted.

Trisha bent over and covered her daughter's ears. "Hey, you guys, there are children in here, you know."

"Sorry, Terrence and Jennifer," Henry said and kissed Jennifer on the forehead when she came and stood next to his chair.

She giggled and ran back to her mother. Then Jennifer plopped herself down next to Trisha's feet and meowed.

Pam looked up suddenly and asked, "How was work?"

"What?" Trisha asked her mother.

"How was work?" Pam repeated.

"I haven't gone to work yet, Mom; it's nine in the morning."

"What?" Pam said and then, "Oh shoot!" glancing back down at the table. "Now whose trump is it?"

"I don't know, bag lady."

"Honey, whose trump?" Pam asked Trisha.

"Dad's," Trisha said.

"Haha!" Henry laughed. "My trump, my trump!"

"Oh, take it then," Pam demanded.

Henry pulled the pile toward himself. Then he leaned over, picked Jennifer up, and set her on his lap. "This is the only lady I want sitting on my lap from now on," he said. "She don't give me no sass."

Jennifer said, "Meow."

"She don't give you no luck neither," Pam said, laying down an ace of hearts and grinning. She pulled Terrence toward her and put him on her lap. But the second she let go, he ran into the other room and turned on the television.

"Oh, that's it, lady!"

"That's right; it's it … because I just won!"

Trisha looked from her old mom's face to her older dad's face and laughed. "How did you two even end up together?"

"Because we love each other," Pam said and leaned across the table to kiss Henry on the lips.

"It's just poker talk," Henry said and tucked a few escapee strands of gray hair behind Pam's ear. Then he kissed her earlobe. Jennifer wiggled free from her grandfather's lap.

"But aren't you playing hearts?" Trisha asked, a bit confused.

Buster, Trisha's husband, came into the kitchen and kissed Trisha. "Good morning, hot mamma," he said.

Trisha blushed.

"Good morning," she answered.

"Look! The J-man put the sun up just for you," Buster said, pointing to the kitchen window at the sun peeking through the branches of the tree Jennifer had been stuck in less than twenty-four hours ago.

"I guess maybe he did," Trisha said, smiling as she looked out the window.

"It's no maybe, sugar-baby," Buster said, pulling his hair back into a ponytail with a twisty tie from the loaf of bread sitting on the counter. Trisha pulled a box of cereal down from the shelf of a cabinet. She yawned, looked out the window again, and poured one bowl of cereal for herself, one for Buster, one for Terrence, and one for Jennifer. Terrence came in from the living room, grabbed his bowl of cereal from the counter, and sat down at the table in front of it. Jennifer grabbed her bowl and set it on the floor.

Trisha looked at Buster and then at Jennifer, who ate from her bowl of cereal on all fours. Trisha sighed. "We're going to have to start making her eat at the table, you know."

"Let her eat where she wants," Henry said, shuffling the deck of cards. "I talked with God, and he don't care."

****

At the age of two, Terrence wandered out of Trisha's sight in the basement of her father's church. And the man who returned the lost child to her was Buster, a kind man three years older than she. He had just recently been saved by the Lord, Jesus Christ, while lying on a cot in cell block D of the Morristown Correctional Facility.

"I thought he was stolen by non-Christian kidnappers," Trisha said, wiping the tears from her eyes and shoving another doughnut hole in her mouth.

"Shame would be the name of that game," Buster said, handing the child to his mother.

Trisha laughed. Buster sat down next to Trisha. And although he was covered from head to toe in tattoos and had a long ponytail and more muscles than she thought it was possible to have at the same time, she found him quite adorable. The two shared day-old doughnuts, orange juice, and parables.

Trisha asked Buster if he knew if doughnuts were really made of dough that came from cows. He laughed and said he didn't know "cows had the brain batter to use an oven." Trisha liked the way Buster talked. Years in the joint had given him both a dialect all his own and complete faith in the power of Jesus Christ, whom Buster referred to as "the J-man."

Trisha and Buster laughed in the basement of that church as Terrence ran circles around the folding chairs and tables. And by the fourth paper cup of orange juice, Buster and Trisha, an even more unlikely couple than Luke and Trisha, were completely in love with one another. Two months later, they were married in that very same church. And three months after that, Trisha was pregnant with Jennifer.

Trisha, Buster, Terrence, and Jennifer lived with Trisha's mother and father in a house the size of a department-store dressing room. Every day, Buster loved Trisha up and down and sideways. And she loved him back and forth and all around.

Trisha's mother, Pam, was retired from the Quiggly-Wiggly where Buster was placed to do his work-release behind the deli counter, slicing meat. He still worked there to this day. Buster also bartended part-time at a bar down the road to help with finances. Trisha's father,

Henry, was the pastor at the church where she met Buster. It was nice for Trisha's parents to have Trisha and Buster and the grandkids all with them in that little house. They seemed to like the company and the help getting in and out of their recliners. Their bones had begun to crack and curl. Trisha had become a caregiver in the truest sense of the word because of the only circumstances she understood. She did not rue or regret. Trisha was thankful for her life in a way that most people would not understand. Trisha was good at taking care of her parents and her kids. And Buster was good at taking care of Trisha and her parents and those kids.

When Trisha was born, her mom was in her late forties and her dad his early fifties. She was the child they had always wanted but were told they would never be able to have. She was a surprise, a miracle, and very possibly a prank phone call from the Lord himself. There were no complications, unless you count going through menopause while raising a toddler, getting ready to retire while raising a teenager, and to put it simply, having nothing in common with a young woman who just so happens to be your only daughter. Trisha was born deaf in her right ear and had developed the habit of literally leaning in to conversations. Because her parents were elderly and in the process of losing their hearing as well, there was a lot of miscommunication as well as polite yelling at one another in her household.

****

"Daddy's here! I wanna get the door!" Terrence yelled suddenly.

Trisha hadn't even heard him knock but looked over to the front door. Sure enough, Luke was standing there, knocking.

"The truck you will. Finish your Frosted Flakes," Trisha said, pointing a finger at her son. Although her parents and her husband used four-letter words, although every conversation Trisha had ever had with Alison had at least ten of them, even though her father, an actual pastor, cursed, Trisha herself had never once used a curse word. Her love for the Lord just wouldn't allow it.

"I will open the door," she said, walking to the front door. She unlocked it and gave Luke a hug.

"Good morning, everyone!" Luke called from Trisha's embrace.

"Daddy!" Terrence screamed, running toward Luke.

Luke picked him up and kissed him on the forehead.

"I just told him he needs to finish his cereal," Trisha explained to Luke.

Luke nodded. "Mom's right, buddy. Finish your cereal. I will come into the kitchen with you. Luke held hands with his son as they walked to the table. Luke helped Terrence back into his chair. Terrence began to eat again but looked at his dad instead of the bowl. So he kept spilling on himself. Jennifer had finished her cereal and was now sitting on Pam's lap. Pam began braiding Jennifer's hair but made sure to complain about her arthritis each time she grabbed a new piece of hair.

"If it hurts, why do you do it?" Henry asked.

"Oh yeah? Are you gonna do it?" Pam said, yanking Jennifer's head backward. Then she added, "Hi, Luke."

"Me-*ooooooooooow*!" Jennifer screamed.

"I'll do it," Luke said, sitting in a chair next to Pam.

Terrence folded his arms and began to pout.

"What's the haps, partner?" Buster said to Luke, setting a cup of coffee and a bowl of cereal at the table in front of him.

"Thanks, Buster," Luke said, taking the brush from Pam and helping Jennifer onto his lap. "Hi, pumpkinface."

She giggled. "Hi, picklehead," she said back. Then she giggled again.

"Hi, poopybrain!" Terrence said, struggling for attention.

"Hi, turkey burger," Luke said to Terrence.

"Don't say poopy," Trisha scolded.

"Poopy," Terrence said again, smiling at his father.

Buster knocked Terrence upside the head for Trisha.

"You listen to your mamma."

Terrence looked like he was about to start crying. But Luke reached across the table and tickled his neck so he laughed instead.

"Don't pout, Terrence," Henry said. "You look like my wife after I beat her in cards."

"Hey, old man," Pam said, throwing a salt shaker that barely missed him.

Henry laughed. Then he shook his head.

"Not too pretty, is it?" Henry asked the crowded kitchen.

"He's a pastor, and he's lying right to your face. Luke, he didn't beat me. He hasn't beat me in four days," Pam told Luke.

Luke changed the subject.

"You want me to braid your hair or put it in a ponytail, sweetie?" Luke asked as he gently brushed Jennifer's thick, curly hair.

"Ponytail," Jennifer said quietly. "No, three ponytails," she corrected.

"How in the heezy you get my girl to say something 'sides a cat noise?" Buster asked, scratching his head. He grabbed a bowl of cereal and sat down next to Luke.

"Maybe magic," Trisha answered for Luke with two pieces of sausage in her mouth as she handed him three rubber bands to use in Jennifer's hair.

"Maybe, sugar butt," Buster said, kissing Trisha on the cheek.

She giggled.

"Braid my hair, too, Daddy," Terrence tried.

"I can't, bud. It's too short. But I can put some gel in it. You want some gel?"

"Not too much, okay. I know he ain't *my* kid. But we ain't got enough closets over here for him to climb in and out of. Wait till we build us up a bigger house," Buster said, slapping Luke on the arm.

"I won't use any more than I use on myself."

"Where's he use gel?" Buster asked Pam.

"Who's Jill, honey?" Trisha asked her husband.

"I said, 'Where's he use gel?'"

"That's what your dad named his penis, dear," Pam said to Trisha.

Henry tried to high-five his wife. But his arthritis had been acting up lately too, so he ended up swatting at her like a bug. She swatted back at him.

Buster shook his head back and forth. Then he looked from his mother- and father-in-law to his wife, and he smiled.

"Okay, hair salon is closed. The casino too. Sausages are ready," Trisha announced, setting down a plateful of what was left of the sausage after she was done cooking and eating it.

CHAPTER 8

There is a girl
who grew without water
or sun or air;
grew up, inside,
and out–
smarted them all;
never asked to be
the only one
who can reach all the boxes
on the top shelf
collecting dust—
all those boxes
with no plans at all,
waiting for her hands,
for someone tall.

What do you do with a body
when
the outside
doesn't match the in
and the inside
never wants to stay in its skin—
stretching like a cat in the sun,

pulled tighter than the casing of a drum
around muscles and bones, and
a million different shades of red,
making her want to smoke cigarettes
instead
of play ball,
making her talented in a way that
no one ever mentions at all?
The poetry of her heart
was a work of art.

But
what kind of body
of evidence
is enough
to support thoughts
and feelings and dreams,
and what types of facts
prove the existence of these things?

" I need a smoke before we go in," Alison said, lighting a cigarette in front of the small coffee shop sandwiched in between a shoe store and a Blockbuster. Her hands were shaking.

"Whatever you need," Big Joe said, standing between Alison and Sarah.

"I am nervous too," Sarah said. "But we have to go in eventually."

"I know," Alison said, taking a long drag and trying to will her heart to beat slower.

A scrawny twelve- or thirteen-year-old shyly made his way toward Alison and Sarah.

"Hey, you think I could bum a smoke?" he asked, squinting up through the sun at Alison and putting his hands deep into his pockets.

"Sure," she answered, handing him a cigarette from her pack.

"And a light?" he said, taking the cigarette and putting it in his mouth.

"Sure." She handed him her lighter.

"Thanks," he said, lighting the cigarette and proudly walking back toward his friends who waited a half a block away. They stood in a circle and passed the cigarette around to one another.

"I don't think that kid was anywhere close to eighteen," Sarah told Alison.

"We started smoking before we were eighteen."

"I wonder why," Big Joe said sarcastically after Alison threw her cigarette.

She took a deep breath and opened the door. The coffee shop was even smaller on the inside than it looked on the outside, only ten square wooden tables with one or two chairs each. It smelled like cigarettes more than coffee. Smoke hung in the air, although no one was smoking at the moment. There was only one person in the entire place.

"That must be him." Alison shrugged as they walked toward a small, stocky man in a stained white T-shirt sitting at a table with two chairs, one of which held his body and the other his feet.

"You must be the people cashing in on Fish's favor," he said, closing a newspaper and glancing up at Sarah, Alison, and Big Joe. Sarah held out her hand. But Anthony didn't take it. Instead, he took a drink from a tiny espresso cup, looked at Alison, and asked, "You looking for the person who beat you up?"

"No, we are looking for this man," she said, handing him the paper with her father's face and information on it. "I also have this," she said, handing him another paper. On it, she had written down as much information as she could about her dad: his license plate, Social Security number, previous places of employment, favorite color, and so on. He looked over the paper. "It's my dad," she added.

A phone on the wall rang. "Excuse me," he said, getting up to answer it.

"Anthony, you need to get your shit together," he said into the receiver. "I'm not about to clean up another mess for you." He paused for a bit and then yelled, "Grow the fuck up for Christ's sake!" and slammed the phone down.

"He said Anthony," Alison whispered to Sarah and Big Joe, who had been told watered-down bits and pieces about what happened on Alison's date, mostly because he kept pressing her about why her face looked the way it did. She would have rather not relived any of those sad details. But there were really so many. And it did feel good to just fucking yell about it for once. So maybe, she might just start yelling about a few more things every now and then. Who knows?

"My fucking kid," Anthony said, walking back to the table. "Can't pass a bar, a broad, or a drug test," he said as he sat back down.

"Your son, his name is Anthony too?" Big Joe asked.

"I'm sorry. Who are you?" Anthony asked, sounding annoyed.

"I'm Big Joe. And I think this girl right here may know your son," he said, putting an arm gently around Alison. Today everyone was treating her like a baby bird. A sick baby bird that just might not make it.

"That so?" Anthony said, looking at Alison.

She nodded her broken beak. Anthony sighed, got up, and went behind the counter by the coffee machines. He returned with a picture. "This the boy who did that to your face?"

She looked at the picture and nodded. "It was an accident though. I mean, he didn't hit me. He just threw me out of the car. I mean, he did elbow me … and I guess he did kick me pretty fucking hard too." Her voice was soft at first but grew with each word as did her posture.

Anthony's face became red, and he began clenching his jaw. He tore off a piece of his newspaper and scrawled something on it. "I don't know where he got that shit. From his shitbag friends probably. I …" He hit his chest hard with his right palm. "… always taught him to respect women." He handed the paper to Big Joe. "This is his address. Do what you feel is right. Just don't break his legs. And don't kill him."

Big Joe put the paper in his pocket. Alison didn't stop him. The part of her that believed in the goodness in each and every person in the world didn't give two shits. *I hope he does hurt him. I hope he has to look at his friends with a face that is covered in scabs and gravel too.* The phone rang again. "I will call you as soon as I find David. Shouldn't take that long," he said, standing up. "Now if you will excuse me, I need to get the phone." He paused for a minute while the phone continued to ring and looked at Alison. "Don't worry; I'm sure your dad is just fine," he said with what seemed to be genuine concern.

****

David had made a nice life for himself in the past five years. It was lonely, he admitted, mostly at night. He didn't have a wife or children or a dog to come home to. But he had overtime. He had found a pretty good job selling used cars to people who couldn't afford to buy new ones. There was a younger girl working in the stockroom who reminded him of Alison. She was thin and funny. She cursed without realizing she had even done it, and she worshiped the ground David walked on. This made him both happy and sad. He missed his family less and less every day. But he knew it would never go away completely. Not often, but sometimes at night, he would drive to Jasper County to quietly catch a glimpse of his family living peacefully without him. Only once did he get out of the car. He walked into the empty video store and picked up all the movies he had rented with his wife and daughters. It was a dumb thing to do. He just wanted to touch the places their hands had touched.

He put the movies down and left as quickly as he had come. "No harm done," he told his pastor, Henry, whom he talked to when he could.

Henry filled him in on how his family was doing, what they looked like, and the funny things they did and said. But today, after taking off his wedding ring for the first time since he had put it on, David felt he had to do one more thing for his family. He went into the stockroom where the girl who reminded him of Alison was showing the rest of the crew how to do a dance called the Macarena.

"Jessie," he said, just as Jessie was stopping to catch her breath.

"Oh, hey, Mr. Robbins!"

"Can you help me with something today?"

"Sure. What do you need?" She fanned her face with the back of her hand.

"Can you help me pick out a car for my daughter?" David knew that they would all drive the car, but Alison was the one who would fall in love with it. He wanted it to be a car that would make her heart smile.

"Hell yeah!" Jessie exclaimed. "Let's get her a fucking Mercedes!"

"Have I told you how much you remind me of Alison?" David asked her on the way to the lot of cars.

After they picked out a car, David went home to call Henry. When Henry answered his phone, David told him what he had done.

"Jesus, David. How are we going to give them a car without them knowing it's from you?"

"I don't know," he said. There was a long silence. "I took off my wedding ring today." David sighed.

Then Henry sighed.

"I am sorry. This whole thing is bigger than the both of us, isn't it?" Henry said.

"I just want them to have a good life without me. I want everyone to just move on without me."

"You have to move on too, you know," Henry told him. "God will forgive you, if you ask him to."

David nodded without saying anything. Then he changed the subject. He wasn't ready to talk about what he figured God must have thought about him.

"How are they really?"

"Beautiful and strong. Your wife ..." Henry paused. "Jean looks just exactly the same. I keep waiting for her to age, but she always looks the same. Trisha says Alison is still pestering all the customers at Doug's and flashing your picture to anyone who will talk to her, but who knows what the hell she's talking about half the time? I don't think even she knows. You know that girl doesn't hear anything but pork frying in a skillet."

David laughed but knew there was probably some truth to what Trisha had told Henry.

He went on, "Sarah's still running through the neighborhood almost every morning as if the devil himself were chasing her."

"I never figured out where she got that from. Jean and I never did anything like that."

"The Lord gives us all a gift." There was another silence. "After the car," Henry continued, "we are going to have to let them move on, just like you said. We are all going to have to move on."

"I know, but—"

"The Lord will show you how."

"Thank you, Henry. Thank you for everything."

"You will find the strength, David. Bye. God bless."

"Bye." David fumbled at the place where his wedding band used to be. *Ghost runner on third finger.* His whole hand looked different without it. And he missed the weight and feel of it. There was, of course, a noticeable tan line circling either (a) his wedding ring finger, (b) failed husband and father, (c) quitter, (d) liar, (e) murderer, or (f) all of the above.

****

David Robbins was a perfectly honest middle-class man with a frame like a weather-beaten farm door. He had hair that came loose like the fur on a cat when he ran his hands through it. His face was like a suitcase that had to be sat on to be latched shut because his teeth were too big for his mouth. If his top lip were a roll shade, it would flip back up when you tried to pull it closed, and his sun-colored smile would come busting in at you. He loved hockey, although he never played. He never played anything except horseshoes and cards and the role of Santa Claus for a month in front of the Big and Tall store, modeling their newest gloves and scarves while ringing a bell. But like most people in Jasper County, David had to leave Trenton to find better work. He got a job at the metal plant forty-five minutes away. He had tried all the jobs in town, even suit jobs. But David always looked funny in a tie, like his head was going to pop off or something. His head and body without a neck were a bit like the circles of a snowman with corn kernels for teeth. He was a man who drank coffee all day long; he brought it into the bathroom with him and into the driver's seat of a car that was too little for him. The coffee rocked and spilled onto his knees, which bumped up against the steering wheel as he drove or on the sleeves of the only winter coat he ever owned as a grown man. "I like this coat," he always said when Jean wanted to take him to get a new one. Whenever she wanted to get him something new, that was what he said. He just wanted everything that was new to be for his wife and children. Like most fathers, he wanted his children to have the things other kids had.

David was afraid of Jean working while she was pregnant. There had already been complications. He didn't want anything to happen to his wife or his daughter. He worked three jobs while Jean's stomach itched and ached and housed their first child. He was working the night Sarah was born; he would have been fired if he had left. Jobs were too scarce. And they had just taken out a second mortgage on the house, the house that Sarah, Alison, and Jean now lived in without him.

Linda called him at the plant to tell him that Jean was going into labor. He told her that he hoped she could hang on until he was done. But he hung up the phone, knowing full well that she would if only she could. He pressed his forehead to the cold metal box hanging on the wall, waiting to roll someone's dime around inside its mouth with its clanking metal tongue. He ran his fingers softly along the numbers of the phone as if they were the pain-stricken features on his wife's face as she pushed their daughter into the world. He put his hand flat on the phone's back after he hung it back up, as if it were Jean's bare back and he were holding her upright in that hospital bed.

"I am here," he said into the back of that phone's neck. His lip was too ashamed to tremble. His eyes were full of tears. He blinked them out. Once. Twice. The third time, he kept them closed. And that time when his eyes clicked shut, he had a tiny dream. He saw Sarah's brand-new red face just as he thought it looked upon entering the world, just as it looked to the stars, who blinked themselves. And for a moment, everything was dark. "I am here," he kept saying over and over again. "I am here." *But he wasn't.*

He went to the hospital right after work. Jean and Sarah were asleep on the hospital bed, comfortably warm with sweat, their faces covered in neon lamplight. Sarah's fists were balled up. Jean's arms were wrapped around Sarah. David lay down on the other side of his wife, put his arms around the both of them, and cried again. It was no time for him to lose any of his jobs. There was a new member now, mortgages, and hospital bills. He had to work. That was what he knew.

He was a father in the sense that he provided for his children. And they did see him at dinnertime and in the early mornings. But somehow, over time, David began to associate being a father with working. The more he worked, the better a father he was because the more money they had as a family. And although his muscles ached and his eyes stung with a tiredness none of them could ever understand, although he hated his jobs, he took pride in the fact that they had everything that they wanted. They had Pop-Tarts and coloring books and a cassette player and new shoes and bikes with colored banana seats and baskets. They *were* happy.

It was true that both Jean and David had thought about a divorce or a separation. But it was not that they spent more time apart than they did together. It was not their failing marriage that made David leave Jean and their children. He loved Jean. He loved Alison and Sarah. He loved James and Luke as if they were his own. After all, he was the closest thing either of them had to a father. He was the only one who could protect them. He was the one who taught them how to be men. He taught them how to play baseball, even if Luke never really learned how to throw overhand. It was David who taught Luke how to run around the bases. But that is not what David did. He did not run. He just got tired of watching that family get hurt. You can only watch for so long. Then one day, you can't take it anymore. You have to do something.

David had talked to Charles plenty of times. He had even roughed him up a few. After that, Charles always stopped. And after a while, he always started back up. Luke wasn't strong enough to do it. Linda wasn't sure enough. James should have done it, probably would have done it, if not for that night it rained harder than steel, the night the sky just opened up and out poured thick wet nails, driving holes into the soft ground, like God was desperately trying to hammer everything down. Or maybe God just wanted to cover up the sound and smell of pain.

Either way, James's father must have been driving home from the bar drunk as the devil, going too fast, driving in the manner in which he walked, swaying from side to side. There was a moment when David found him leaning on the side of a car smashed into a tree with blood running down his face and arms and he saw a man, just a regular man, like himself, a man who had missed all the important things and hated himself for it. But that moment faded when Charles noticed David shut his car door and walk toward him.

"What the fuck you doing out here, David?"

"Was just on my way home. Looks like you could use some help."

"I don't need a fucking thing, big man," he said, still leaning on the car. He pulled out a cigarette and a lighter and began trying to light it.

David thought about the man Charles was, the way he treated his family, the kids who had become best friends with his own.

"You want to kick my ass again, don't you?" he slurred. "Do it. I don't even care anymore. I know you think I'm a piece of shit. Bet you wish I would've died when I ran into this tree, huh?" He finally got his cigarette lit and took a big drag.

"Let's just get you home," he said, approaching Charles and trying to help him to stand upright.

"Fuck you," he slurred, pushing David's arms off of him.

David stepped away from Charles and stood there for a minute. Just a minute. Then he went to the passenger side of the smashed car, opened the door and the glove box, and took out the gun that he knew Charles kept there. David shut the door and came around to the driver's side of the car where Charles was just leaning, doing nothing good like he had done nothing good for so many years. If Charles had done anything, just one thing … If he had looked like he gave a shit or talked about why he was the way he was, anything, to make David understand or care about a man who hurt people for no reason. But he just leaned on that driver's side door, smoking his cigarette. Charles watched as David switched off the safety and raised the gun. Charles laughed.

"Them kids never deserved you," David said and shot Charles in the heart.

The color and expression on Charles's face changed from hard to soft. "Probably true," Charles said, slowly sliding down the car to sit.

"Can you get me that bottle of whiskey in the backseat?" he asked, putting a hand over the blood that was coming out slowly at first but then quickly. David opened the door back up and grabbed the bottle. He brought it to Charles, who took a large pull.

"You good now?"

"Yeah, David. I'm good. Tell them I'm sorry."

"Who?"

"Everyone," he said, taking another drink. "I never meant to be like this."

"I know." David put the gun back up and shot Charles again in the same place. It felt like putting down a sick dog because you didn't want it to hurt anymore—and you didn't want it hurting anyone else either. He did it partly because he couldn't understand why God wanted such a bad man to live in the first place, a man who hurt and hated and took up space. There are some people who are meaner than dogs. But also David did it because he understood what it felt like not to know anything about your family and hate yourself for it.

It was true that Charles didn't remember half the things he said or did clearly enough to feel guilty about them. It was like he had amnesia. This is how it is with alcoholics. But forget something once, and it will forgive you. Forget something too many times, and it will forget you too. Only the stars could tell you in their beautiful, blinking Morse code that David didn't plan on shooting Charles. But he did it just the same. After Charles died, David picked him up and put him back into his smashed-up car.

Maybe Cassiopeia, who just happens to be sitting overhead, will comfort me, give me a sign that it was neither accident nor murder; it was sorrow. It was those words, "I am sorry," that stopped Charles's heart because he meant them. Maybe he meant them more than he had ever meant anything in his life. To not only feel them but to say them as he felt them at the same time, well, Charles's heart just wasn't strong enough for that. David looked up at the stars. He waited for one to fall so that he could make a wish. He didn't want to take it back. But he didn't want to be responsible for taking another life. The stars didn't fall, didn't blink, or even flinch. He got into his car and drove home to his family.

CHAPTER 9

Sometimes okay
doesn't really mean
okay.
If you flip it over,
open up the letters,
and wipe off the dirt,
you can see inside
all the compartments
stuffed with guilt
and
hurt
and
pain—
secrets
piled on top
of secrets,
all sticky;
you
can't separate them
or shake them,
can't pour them out
of your brain or your mouth,
can't get them out

because they cling
like a tick you have to burn.
Part will always stay
stuck under the skin;
its body will be gone
except for the part that got in

side

out

side in.

Okay

is really just

a bunch of loser

letters

pretending to

win.

"I t's about God damn time!" Little Joe yelled at Big Joe as he walked in through the kitchen door in front of Alison and Sarah. The three of them were almost an hour late for work. "What the …" he stopped yelling when he saw Alison's face. "Everyone okay?"

"Yep," Big Joe said, grabbing an apron from the counter and putting it on. "But we got something to take care of after work tonight."

Little Joe nodded. "Well, don't worry; Doug ain't in yet."

"Thanks, Little Joe," Sarah said.

"And thanks, Big Joe," Alison added as the two of them left the kitchen and headed toward the dining room.

There was no time to catch up. It was busy. And with only Luke, James, and Trisha working, things had piled up quickly. Trisha gave Alison half of her tables, and Luke gave Sarah half of his tables plus a new one—the Grangers.

****

In Jasper County, most people were afraid of the house that belonged to the Grangers. This was the house that all the kids skipped when they went trick-or-treating on Halloween for fear that a real witch might answer the door. This was the house that was surrounded by the yard that kids in the neighborhood sure as shit didn't step foot in when they walked to school. It was the yard with the dog that kids didn't make eye contact with, even though he was chained to a tree because they were afraid he would pull it out of the ground, chase them down, tear off all their limbs, and bury the bones.

The Grangers were the town's meanest, angriest husband and wife. They hated company and conversation, and most of all, they hated one another. Yet they remained unhappily married for forty years.

Mrs. Granger had her hair pulled back so tightly that her crow's-feet looked like they extended into her hair and met each other at the back of her head underneath her French braid. Her teeth were stained with lipstick. She was furiously smoking a cigarette and batting it against the plastic ashtray so vehemently that the cherry kept coming off. When it did, she rolled her eyes and relit the cigarette. Mr. Granger sat with his arms tightly folded and unfolded them only long enough to swish her smoke away from his face.

"Where in the hell is our waitress?" Mr. Granger asked, looking around.

Alison nudged Sarah and pointed to the Grangers.

"I know. I know." Sarah sighed. She passed Trisha on her way to the table. "Tell God to quit testing me," she said angrily.

"What?"

"Nothing."

****

"It's like they forgot about us or something. The food is probably going to take forever," Mrs. Granger added.

"Oh, I'm sure it will," Mr. Granger confirmed.

When Sarah approached them, Mr. Granger said, "Finally," and swatted his wife's smoke into Sarah's face.

Sarah coughed.

"Oh great, our waitress has a cold," Mrs. Granger said, shaking her head back and forth in disgust.

Sarah shook her head back and forth with more disgust.

"No, it's the smoke you just swatted into my face."

"Well, if we hadn't been waiting for a half an hour—" Mr. Granger started.

But Sarah cut him off.

"My name is Sarah."

"Well, Tara, can we get some menus?" Mrs. Granger asked, annoyed.

"The person who sat you here didn't give you any menus?" Sarah asked, knowing full well they didn't wait to be seated as the sign at the front door so politely asked. She saw them read it and then walk right past and plop down at her table. "I am sorry," she said. But she wasn't. "I will get you some. And my name is Sarah, not Tara."

"Jesus Christ," Mrs. Granger said, smashing her cigarette into the ashtray.

Sarah returned with the menus, which Mr. and Mrs. Granger immediately snatched from her hands.

"Can I get you something to drink?"

"Well, we haven't looked at the menus yet, remember?"

"Okay," Sarah said and walked away. She was not sticking around for more.

As soon as she got to another table, Mrs. Granger started waving her arm at Sarah. "Excuse me; can I have a glass of water?" she called loudly.

"I'm sorry," Sarah said to her new customers.

They smiled sympathetically at her.

"Go ahead," someone at the table told Sarah.

Sarah immediately liked them.

"I'll be right back," she said and walked back over to the Grangers.

"I'll have a coffee," Mr. Granger blurted, handing Sarah the ashtray.

"Okay."

"I'll have a burger, but I don't want it too well done. You always cook them too well. And I don't want the fries so salty. But make sure they're crispy. They are usually soggy," Mrs. Granger said, holding her menu out for Sarah to take.

Mr. Granger continued to look over his menu.

"I'm not ready yet. You didn't give me enough time," he said.

"Okay, I will be back," she told them and went to the bar where James gave her free beer to give to the table that had so graciously waited until the Grangers were done bossing her around.

****

"This water tastes bad," Mrs. Granger said and slid her glass to the edge of the table.

"I guess I'll have a burger too. I don't know why, though. Your burgers are always burnt to a crisp. And a water," Mr. Granger said.

"Okay." She took his menu from him.

"Can I have an ashtray?" Mrs. Granger said, lighting another cigarette. Then she added, "Unless you just want me to ash my cigarette on the floor."

"Okay."

As Sarah walked away, Mrs. Granger shouted, "And new water!" at the back of her head.

When Sarah brought their food out, Mr. Granger said, for the second time, "Finally."

"Well, they look soggy. Of course, they are covered in salt, too," Mrs. Granger said when Sarah put her plate in front of her.

"There is no salt on them, Miss."

"Please don't call me 'Miss.' I am married," she said, holding up her ring.

"Okay."

Sarah said okay because it was a safe word. It was not fishy or fancy. It did not do dances or laps or photo shoots. It was mediocre. If it were a drink, it would be a club soda, without a lime. If it were a snack, it would be celery or crackers but not both at once. If it were a profession, well, it would be a waitress. Okay did not lean one way or the other. It was impartial. It did not insinuate *my pleasure* or *go fuck yourself.* It simply said okay. Sarah hated the Grangers. But she wasn't allowed to hate them. She was paid by them to serve them. So she simply said okay.

Sarah ran into Luke in the kitchen. "Saw you got stuck with the Grangers." He gave a little shiver and said, "They used to scare the holy crap out of me when we were little."

"Luke, the Grangers could scare the holy crap out of Big Joe."

"That I doubt," he said. "Unless ..." He paused, smiling bigger and bigger. Sarah could tell where this was going. "Unless Mrs. Granger showed Big Joe her tits."

"That's disgusting."

"Aw, tits are tits," Big Joe called from the fryer.

Luke made a gagging sound.

When Sarah returned to the Grangers' table to ask how everything was, Mrs. Granger made a face that looked like it was trying to adjust to the taste of expired milk.

"Awful," Mr. Granger answered, taking a bite of his pickle.

"Even the pickle?" Sarah tried.

"Yes, even the pickle," he said before taking another bite and letting the juice run down his chin.

"Okay," she said.

Luke was at a table of three women. Sarah could not see them, but she could tell they were women by the way they were laughing. She heard Luke say, "Who me?" Then she heard the ladies start laughing even harder.

When Sarah walked back into the kitchen, she saw that Trisha had been made a judge in a who-can-say-the-alphabet-fastest contest between the Joes, probably involuntarily. No matter how fair or impartial you remained as a judge in any of their contests, one of them always ended up saying you were against them. When Sarah asked Little Joe how he got Trisha to agree to be a judge, he said he told her she could have as many mozzarella sticks as she wanted while she judged. So there she stood, watching the clock on the wall as Little Joe rattled off twenty-six letters as fast as he could. Then he took a drink of water, which it appeared Trisha was including in his time.

"Nineteen seconds. Great job," she said, dipping a mozzarella stick in mayonnaise. She shoved the whole thing into her mouth.

"Hey, guys," Sarah started to say but was cut off when Big Joe put up his hand and spit out the ABCs in ten seconds flat.

Sarah rolled her eyes. "I just need—"

Big Joe held up his hand again and waited for Trisha's official time.

"No, no, no, you forgot the letter Q!" Little Joe shouted.

"No, I didn't," he dismissed Little Joe. "How long?" he asked Trisha, who looked like she might have forgotten to count. "Fifteen seconds," she said and swallowed a glob of fried cheese.

"Doesn't count. You forgot Q."

"Did I forget Q?" Big Joe asked Sarah.

"I just need a salad with no tomatoes," she tried.

"Q or no Q?" Big Joe asked with a very serious face.

"No Q," she said because she needed her salad and Little Joe was in charge of the salads.

"Here you go, beautiful," Little Joe said, plucking the tomatoes from a salad and handing it to her.

"Thanks," she said and quickly headed toward the swinging door.

"This is re-dic-u-lous!" Big Joe shouted. "I didn't forget Q!"

"Thanks for the mozzarellas," Trisha said before shoving the last two pieces into her mouth and leaving the kitchen.

****

The lunch rush ended, giving way to the best part of the day, the part when the staff was able to sit in the parking lot on lawn chairs, smoke cigarettes, eat leftovers, and talk. The kitchen door's mouth was wide open. And the kitchen exhaled its fiery wing sauce and salted fish breath into the air.

As usual, Trisha went home to her family while James, Luke, Alison, Big Joe, Little Joe, and Sarah sat on the lawn chairs that were arranged in a circle. Their aprons lay on the ground in a pile by the door. Sarah took off her socks and shoes and slid them under her chair. She pulled up her pant legs as far as they would go and put her sweaty bare feet on the arm of Big Joe's chair. She leaned her head back and felt the heavy, thick breeze on her face. She watched James count the freckles on her sister's face.

"Any new ones?" Alison asked, squinting at him through the sun.

"How'd you know what I was doing?"

"I could feel your eyes. Plus you tap your foot when you count, remember?"

"You don't know what I was counting though."

"Freckles," she answered. Alison barely even brushed her hair in the morning, let alone put on makeup. Her soft freckles were left free and uncovered on her face.

"I think you are a psychic."

"Alison saw a psychic once," Luke said, doing a triple jump right into their conversation.

"I did," Alison said, sitting up in her chair. "At the county fair."

"Can we quit avoiding the elephant in the parking lot?" Sarah asked suddenly. She could not take the fact that no one had mentioned anything that had happened in the past twenty-four hours.

"I was waiting for Alison to bring it up," James said, looking at Alison.

"Okay, fine, recap," Alison said, getting up from her chair and pretending to hold a clipboard. "Item number one," she said, pretending to be reading from her clipboard. "I got beat up on my date last night. As a side note, this has happened before," she whispered, cupping one of her hands around the side of her mouth. "Item number two, the guy I went on a date with has a hit man father who is okay with us kicking his son's ass as long as we don't kill him or break his legs. Item number three," she said, holding up three fingers with her left hand as she continued to hold the fake clipboard with her right hand. "He is going to help us find Dad but not to kill him." She pretended to look for more items on the clipboard but find nothing. "Meeting adjourned," she said, pretending to throw the imaginary clipboard up in the air and shoot it with an imaginary rifle.

"What?" Little Joe and Luke said simultaneously.

"Actually that's pretty much it," Sarah said.

"How did you find a hit man?" Little Joe asked.

"A guy named Fish," James answered.

"So his son was the same guy you went out with?" Luke asked.

"Yep," Alison answered, sitting back down in her chair.

Sarah could see Alison becoming a glimpse of the person she was that morning, tearing her room apart, heaving, and screaming. There was a look of anger in her eyes with the sound of frenzied resentment in her voice. Alison, the girl who asked her sister not to go after the boy who raped her in high school, the girl who felt bad for hot dogs, the girl who thought everyone deserved a chance or two or twenty seemed to be fading. And it hurt Sarah's heart.

"Okay, I just wanted to make sure we were all up to speed. Meeting adjourned," Sarah said. She wanted to ask the new Alison to bring back the old Alison.

"So what are we going to do to the guy?" James asked the Joes.

"We said meeting adjourned!" Alison yelled as she stood back up, flipped over her chair, and went inside.

James stood up to follow her, but Sarah put her arm out and stopped him. "Give her some space. I will go in there and see how she is in a minute."

"Okay," he said, sitting back down.

Sarah saw Big Joe show Little Joe the newspaper with Anthony's address on it. They talked in hushed voices until Little Joe caught Sarah watching them. He nudged Big Joe, who put the paper back in his pocket and leaned back in his chair. But before he did Sarah heard him say the name Steven Segal and something about being "Out for justice."

Little Joe took off his shirt, revealing medium-sized nipples and medium-sized shoulders. He threw it into the pile of aprons and shoes. In response, Big Joe took off his shirt, revealing rows upon rows of muscles that bulged and pumped even when he sat perfectly still, and threw it on top of Little Joe's.

"Ha," was all he said.

Little Joe rolled his eyes.

Their relationship always reminded Sarah of two dogs. Whenever they fought, you were nervous. But there was a lightheartedness to it, a laugh or a soft punch that let you know they were just playing. Three months ago, James had the Joes over to watch a ball game. James told everyone that instead of watching the game, the two Joes spent three and a half hours trying to see who could eat more Habanero peppers without crying, punching each other in the stomach as hard as they could, and seeing who could chug more beer. Needless to say, both Joes called in to work the next day and Doug had to cook. The restaurant only sold fried food and soup that day because Doug didn't know the first thing about cooking for people. It was a busy lunch. Doug couldn't keep up with all the orders that were coming in. And it looked to his employees like Doug had to keep shoving french fries in his mouth to keep from crying.

"I'm going to see if anyone's waiting for service in there," Luke announced, getting up from his chair.

Sarah looked up at him.

"I'll check on her," he told her before she could even ask.

The rest of the group didn't even flinch. Sarah closed her eyes and pretended to be asleep so that she could think. James, too, closed his eyes and let his arms hang loose over the sides of his chair. But Sarah figured the thoughts running around in his head probably wouldn't let him sleep either.

"Car!" Little Joe yelled, popping up from his chair and leaning to see around the dumpster. None of them wanted Doug to round the corner and catch them in the middle of their porch party. This was their midafternoon secret. They had kept it between themselves for years, guarded it with their lives. It was their buried treasure. And they were very careful not to let Doug take it from them.

"Never mind. It's a truck," Little Joe said, sitting back down.

"Jackass," Big Joe said, throwing his hat at Little Joe.

"At least I'm paying attention," Little Joe defended himself, throwing the hat back.

****

When Luke came back outside, Alison was with him. Her face was puffy but dry. He gave her hand a little squeeze before they went to separate chairs and sat down.

"No customers. We may as well just flip the sign to closed so we don't have to keep checking."

Every time they sat out back by the dumpster, someone suggested flipping the sign. But for some reason, they never did. Maybe they were scared of "officially" breaking the rules. Maybe they secretly respected Doug, or at least his business. Maybe they just didn't mind getting up and checking every now and then, because, frankly, most of them never had to get up at all. Luke volunteered every time.

****

Perhaps it was because Luke had thought he let his own mother down, perhaps it was because he was small or gay or the only person in town not the color of white trash that he did whatever anyone asked. Back when Luke first moved to Jasper County, the children asked him to do all the things they couldn't get away with. After all, he was too small and cute to be held accountable for his actions. They had no idea he was seven. They thought four, maybe five. So did everyone else. Their favorite game was the piss-on-this game. At first, Alison and Sarah just wanted to see a penis and James wanted to see a black one. But from the first time Alison pointed to the mailbox and Luke angled his dark little inchworm up at the place where their mailwoman would soon put her hands, they realized they had something. Luke would let them know when he had to go to the bathroom, pull down his pants, and start to pee. The object was to get as many things peed on as possible.

"Pee on that ant," Sarah said.

Luke peed on the ant.

"No, that's mean," Alison said. "Pee on the basketball."

Luke peed on the basketball. It rolled down the driveway. And they cracked up.

"Pee on that truck tire," James said.

Luke peed on the truck tire.

"Pee on Alison's foot," Sarah said.

"No!" Alison yelled, hopping from one foot to the other.

"I can't. I got no more pee," Luke said.

Alison breathed a sigh and stopped hopping.

"Oh wait ... I got a little left," Luke said and peed on Alison's foot.

"Hey!" Alison screamed.

"They told me," Luke defended himself. And he was absolutely right; they had told him. She couldn't argue with that. Their record was twelve but would have been fifteen if Alison hadn't made the rule that Luke wasn't allowed to pee on anything living. (Contrary to popular belief, this wasn't a rule that was formulated after the foot episode. It was enacted one day when he took down an innocent butterfly with his semiautomatic penis.) Pretty much anything in the driveway, street, or yard had been peed on within a month. The novelty wore off, and they created a new game. Luke liked to sing so they set him in front of the general store and made him sing "Yankee Doodle Dandy." Sometimes people would pat him on the head; other times, people would give him a nickel or, if they were lucky, a quarter. Again the novelty wore off. But there was always another game to be created. The deal was as long as it didn't cause physical pain, he would do whatever they asked. And they would never hurt him anyway. They beat the living crap out of each other, but Luke, they would never hurt. All he ever wanted in the world was to make them happy and to make them laugh. And he did. So he was granted immunity. The only person to ever hurt that boy was James's father.

****

Buster waited until Pam and Henry had gone out to sit on the porch and the children were in the middle of their nap. He pulled an envelope out of his jeans pocket and sat down at the kitchen table. Inside that envelope was Buster's crime. He sighed. "I'm sorry, J-man. Them girls are good girls. Henry says I am doing this for them." He looked at the fake scratch tickets he made at the Kinko's in another town, not the Kinko's in the town he used to work at, the one where he was cuffed and read his rights in the middle of a shift-change, but a different Kinko's, in a different town. They were tricky to get right, at first. But Buster had been replicating them now for five years. They looked exactly the same as the real tickets. Across the top, they each said *"Mega Bucks"* in the exact type and color. They were the same size and texture and glossy shine and weight. They were, in fact, exactly the same as the real tickets, if not for one minor inconsistency; these tickets were all guaranteed winners. There was movement in the room where the kids were napping. Buster quickly sealed the envelope and put it back in his pocket as he heard the front door open.

"Honeytoosh!" Buster said to Trisha as she walked into the kitchen.

"Hi, sweetheart. I was just missing you," Trisha said, coming up to him and giving him a big hug.

"I been missing you all day. I brought you home a present from work today," he said. He got up, went to the refrigerator, and pulled out a plastic bag. She took the bag, untied the knot, and looked inside.

"Meat!" she squealed. "Oh, baby, you are so sweet!"

"There was this cat buying flowers for his lady at the grocery store today, and it got me thinking, I oughta get a little trick or treat for my queen a' Sheba too. I didn't get you flowers 'cuz you can't eat 'em. But if you want, I can get you some."

"No, no, baby, this is exactly what I wanted." She kissed him all over his face and neck. "What did I ever do to deserve you?"

"Vice that verse," Buster said, tilting his head and smiling. He whacked her on the butt as she bent over to put the meat back into the refrigerator. When she turned around, he pretended to shake a pair of dice, blow on them, and throw them at her.

"Maybe I should go ahead and have some now, you know, before the kids wake up."

"Have some, babe. It's for you."

She smiled and opened back up the refrigerator.

"Lordy, girl, you eating again?" Henry called as he walked in the front door.

"Don't say—"

"I know, I know. Don't say 'Lord' unless you're talking to the Lord. You know what, Trisha? I am a pastor. That means I can say *damn* and *poop* and *Lord Jesus Christ* whenever I please. Okay?"

Trisha scowled.

"Oh snap," Buster said.

****

Jean was sitting in front of the TV, watching *Days of Our Lives* when her stomach began to grumble. "Stop that," she said, looking down at her own stomach.

Bob must have thought she was talking to him because his tail started wagging. He looked up at her.

"Not you," she said, pointing at Bob. "You," she said, pointing at her stomach. "We are waiting for the girls," she said, this time neither to her stomach nor to Bob but to the television set, more specifically, Dedra Hall. "We'll just wait a little longer," she said to Dedra, who was, in this particular episode, possessed by the devil. Just after Dedra was successfully—Jean crossed her fingers—exorcized, she got up and went into the kitchen. She was planning on making egg-salad sandwiches.

She set everything that she would need out on the counter—eggs, mayo, salt, pepper, bread, and butter. Then she returned to the living room and sat back down on the carpet across from Dedra.

****

Jean stood in the kitchen in front of the counter, looking at the eggs. She tapped her fingernails on the counter. "I guess they didn't have time to come home for lunch," she said sadly to the eggs, mayo, salt, pepper, bread, and butter. But before she honestly let herself believe it, she went outside and walked to the end of the driveway. She looked down the road to see if she could spot her girls in the distance walking home. She stood there a minute. Waiting. One more minute. Waiting. One. More. Minute. Then she went inside, put all the extra bread and eggs away, and made herself a sandwich.

****

"Fuck!" Alison cried suddenly, sitting straight up in her chair. Her face was flushed and guilty. "It's Tuesday!" she exclaimed quickly and loudly in the same voice you would use if you had just gotten kicked right between the ribs.

"Oh crap," Sarah said, heaving a sigh.

On Tuesdays, Jean always finished work early. Sarah and Alison always came home to have lunch with her. To a regular person, egg-salad sandwiches with her children probably wouldn't be that big of a deal. But to Jean, it was a very big deal. Jean had always been the type who desperately tried to please others. Maybe it was because her husband was the first person to tell her "Good job" that she married him. Maybe. But then again, all people like to hear they are good at something. Jean was sensitive. By not coming home or calling, they had hurt her feelings. Both Alison and Sarah knew it.

"I'll go call her," Sarah said, getting up from her chair.

When her mom picked up the phone, she was chewing on mashed-up eggs.

"I'm sorry," Sarah spouted before Jean could swallow and say hello. "We were really busy today."

"That's what I figured," Jean answered. "It's okay," she said. And that was what Sarah knew she would say. Jean had trouble standing up for herself. She would never say, "No, it's not okay. You hurt my feelings."

Even though she said it was okay, Sarah knew it was not okay. Sarah shook her head from side to side. *No, it's not okay to forget about people.*

"I'm really sorry we didn't make it."

"It's okay, José. I am just eating a sandwich. David and I are watching the soap. We're having a good time together," she said.

Sarah could hear her chewing up the eggs and bread over the phone.

"Um, well, I better go. Have a good day."

"Oh, I will. Me and David are just about to go outside and plant some flowers," Jean said.

Sarah bit her lip. She knew that whenever her mom was upset, she planted flowers.

"I am sorry if you were waiting for us. We should have called. I will see you tonight. Okay? I love you, Mom."

"I love you too, Cutie Poo."

"Bye," Sarah said.

"I love you," Jean said again.

"I love you too, Mom. Bye." Sarah hung up the phone before her mother could say, "I love you," again. She noticed a customer sitting at the bar, waiting for a drink. "Hi!" she called as she hung up the phone. "Can I get you a beer?"

"I'll take a Miller Lite."

"No problem." She poured a Miller Lite and put it in front of him. "You want a menu?"

"Sure. I'm just killing some time," he said.

Sarah handed him a menu and went back outside.

"She'll be okay," Sarah told Alison. "We'll call her again later. She'll like that." She didn't tell Alison that their mom was going to plant flowers. It would have just made her feel worse.

"Okay," Alison said, looking like she felt just as guilty as Sarah did.

"You've got a customer," Sarah said to James. "He's just drinking a beer. He might need to get something to eat."

"Should I go back in and talk to him?"

"Yes," Alison said vehemently. "No one wants to eat lunch all by themselves." She looked at Sarah. Sarah did not look at her. But she could feel Alison's sad little eyes on her.

****

Jean always thought that if her husband were to come back home in the summertime, he wouldn't recognize his house. Their once-rotten yard with its bald patches and dried brown grass had evolved into a soft-colored canvas. All the edges and corners were filled with different-colored plants and flowers. It was beautiful. And it was only one of Jean's forms of therapy. After the disappointment of eating alone, Jean finished off the rest of her stash of ditch weed, knowing that her dealer, the town paperboy, would be there soon. She went to the grocery mart, only slightly stoned, and bought a pallet of flowers. She rested on her knees next to the mailbox, which was already surrounded by all the plants and petals of the rainbow. She dug a hole the size of the one in her heart and shoved life into it. Bob lay on his back next to Jean, wrapped in a blanket of sun, and caught himself a doggy-style tan. "You are beautiful," she said to each flower as she moved it from its plastic holder into its new home in her yard. Jean may have been more stoned than she thought because as she was patting the dirt firm against the roots of a red begonia, it whispered, "So are you, Ms. Robbins. So are you."

****

The paperboy arrived on Jean's doorstep, acne popping and gum chomping, with her newspaper and, more important, a plastic baggy that looked like crispy green oregano mixed with mouse turds and smelled like Bob Marley's ancestors. She smiled. He smiled. His pimples and craters stretched. He held out the baggy first.

"Oh, put it in the newspaper for goodness' sake," she said, scanning the street and sidewalk for a curious news reporter who may have somehow gotten lost in her little town.

"Sorry." He shrugged and dropped the baggy into the hole of the rolled newspaper. It slid through and landed on Jean's bare foot.

"Oh for goodness' sake, Jake," she said, picking up the baggy and putting it in her pocket.

"My name's Chris."

"I know, Joe," she said, taking the newspaper. "I can't find my pipe. Do you think I could have a couple zigzigs?"

"You mean zigzags, Mrs. Robbins?" he asked arrogantly.

"You know those things you roll up the marijuana in," she explained, whispering the word *marijuana* and covering it up with her hand.

"I know what you mean," he said in his prepubescent, pimpled voice. "Here," he said, handing her a tiny white box.

"Oh goody. Thank you, sweetheart." She handed him thirty dollars and winked. She always winked like she was in the middle of some big drug ring or something, like she hadn't just been completely ripped off by a seventh-grader, like she was ripping *him* off. And, in a way, she always kind of felt like she was. "Are you sure it's only thirty dollars?"

"Yeah, just thirty, Mrs. Robbins. Hell of a deal, huh?"

"Don't say 'hell,' sweetie. But you're right. Heck of a deal. Here, take five dollars for the zigzigs, okay?"

"Okay. Thanks," he said, shaking his head bewilderedly.

Like taking candy from a baby, she thought as she closed the door.

****

Jean did not smoke pot to get stoned the way you do in high school and college. In fact, she never even smoked *cigarettes* in high school. And she never went to college. It wasn't until after her husband left that she started smoking cigarettes. And it wasn't until after she started smoking cigarettes that she tried pot. After David left her, she tried desperately to forgive herself for somehow making him leave and to forgive him for leaving. It was only two years ago that Alison suggested to her mother that she try smoking pot to numb the pain. It was with Alison that Jean tried pot for the first time. And Alison tried it for either the sixty-fifth time or the seventy-second time, depending on whether or not you count brownies and birthday cakes.

There they sat, on the back porch, like some kind of mixed-up made-for-TV movie, crazy mother and hippy daughter, smoking weed as the sun bled right through the clouds like they were nothing but shredded generic tampons. The June bugs smacked their backs up against the screen windows.

"You might not get high the first time," Alison explained, licking the thin paper to seal a joint that could enter a Virginia Slim look-alike contest and win runner-up, at least. It was a mother's joint, Alison thought triumphantly, as she sealed the paper tightly together with her thumb and pointer finger. "But maybe you will. This is pretty good shit."

"Don't say 'shit,'" Jean scolded and pursed her lips.

"Okay, Mom."

"Okay," Jean repeated back.

"So you don't smoke it like a cigarette. You smoke it like this," Alison instructed. "Like you mean business." Alison lit the jay and sucked hard so that the paper made a crunching sound as it burned.

"Then you hold it in," she added, demonstrating by sitting up straight and looking squarely at her mom as she passed her the joint. Jean did as she was told and coughed. And coughed. And coughed.

"Jeeze Louise!" Jean said in between wheezes.

"That means you are doing it right. You got a big hit there, Mom." Alison's tone was one that should have been used by a kindergarten teacher for praising five- and six-year-olds not for encouraging her own mother to smoke weed. But it fit. Jean looked, among other things, slightly and surprisingly proud of herself. Alison took another hit and then passed it back.

"How long have you been smoking pot?"

"A while," Alison said vaguely.

"Seriously?" Jean inquired, forgetting to "puff, puff, pass."

"Yeah, since high school."

"I am a terrible mother," Jean said, coughing afterward.

"You are the opposite of a terrible mother," Alison said softly, taking the joint from her mom. Jean tilted her head to the side, thought for a moment, and then looked at Alison with a confused expression.

"I am a wonderful father?" Jean asked, raising her voice an octave.

Alison burst into laughter. Then Jean burst too. When they both calmed, Alison said, "Yes, you are." She stubbed out the joint and asked, "Are you high?"

"Um, I don't know. Am I?" Jean asked, feeling her forehead with the back of her hand.

"Not hot," Alison said, laughing, "*high*."

"I know," Jean tried. "I was just checking to see if I was hot. I thought maybe I was hot." They both laughed hysterically for a good two hours, or what seemed like two hours. You know, you can never really tell when you're stoned.

CHAPTER 10

Sarah liked to think of her legs
as a run-on sentence
that circled the entire neighborhood—
so many twists and turns,
like a salty pretzel,
no one could have understood
how she ended up in this place
or how this place ended up
with her in it.
A laminated play on words,
a metaphor that's for the birds,
a cat treat strong enough for a dog,
a "tag … you're it"
right in the middle
of someone else's leap frog.
But she would not be the second person
in her family to let go
before it was
her turn,
which she hoped
would come
soon.

Each time she felt too tired
to solve another problem,
to fix another mistake,
tape together something she didn't break,
she looked up at the moon.
"I can't fix everyone
all the time.
Please,
give me just one minute
that is all mine."

"My husband is the sweetest person God ever made," Trisha said loudly to the whole restaurant as she walked through the front door. Luckily, there weren't many patrons at the moment.

"Why's that?" Luke asked.

"Welllllll … He gives me presents."

"What did he give you?" James asked.

"Four pounds of hard salami."

There was a rumble of laughter coming and going in every direction.

"What's so funny?" Trisha asked.

"Sounds like a penis," Luke explained and patted Trisha on the back.

"What!" she shrieked. "He gave me salami, hard salami. How does that sound like a man's thing?"

"You know what a salami looks like before it's cut, right?" Luke explained further. "And what's a penis do when it gets excited?"

You could see Trisha putting it all together in her head. "Oh dear," she said, getting red in the face. "I am not talking about his private part," she declared to the restaurant.

Trisha was making her announcement as Alison was walking out of the kitchen.

"What's she preaching about now?" Alison asked Sarah.

"Buster's gift," Sarah said.

Alison nodded. "I've heard that before," she said.

While Trisha was distracting the restaurant with her inability to decipher analogies relating to male genitalia, Josie and Bob were seated at one of Sarah's tables. They were discussing the whereabouts of a large sum of money. They stopped when Sarah got close. But before they did, she could have sworn she heard her name.

"Who are you two telling secrets about over here?"

"Oh, I'm just telling her about some criminals," Bob tried.

"Criminals?" Sarah asked suspiciously. "In Jasper County? You mean like jaywalkers and litterbugs?"

Bob and Josie laughed nervously. "Do either of you want another drink?"

"No, thanks. We'd better go," Bob said quickly.

"I got my eye on you two," Sarah said, tapping her pen on their table. And as she walked away, this time, she knew she heard her name.

****

Before Sarah had the chance to ask James what he thought Josie and Bob may have been talking about, a group of men sat down at the bar and began ordering beers. She waited for him to finish getting their drinks. But then a mob of loud women came in and sat at the bar. Sarah knew that she was going to have to wait even longer because these women, who were at least twice James's age, were regulars and were very interested in him. They leaned their cleavage over the bar at him, smoked their cigarettes, and leafed through the bar's only book of song requests for karaoke. They licked their index fingers and flipped through the book. These women sang the same songs every time they came in and always debated on whether or not to sing something different but never did.

"You gonna do Dolly tonight?" one lady yelled to another.

"I will if you will," the other lady answered.

They crashed Bloody Mary glasses and then took simultaneous sips. The lady who initially asked about Dolly added loudly, "I'm just going to try and sing 'Jolene' this time!"

Some other ladies who weren't with the mob laughed. Everyone knew she wasn't going to just try anything. She sang that song every time, probably rehearsed it at home. She had a choreographed dance. Alison and Sarah, who were dumping ice into the beer sink for James, had heard and seen her do it every Tuesday for as long as she had been coming in.

"Shots!" exclaimed the lady who worked at the bank. She was wearing a business suit and matching pumpkin-colored lipstick on both her lips and on her crooked teeth.

James rolled his eyes. Sarah handed him a bottle of apple pucker. He poured four shots of green syrup and set them in front of the pumpkin lady.

"Hey, Handsome," the pumpkin lady's heavy-set friend said to James. She too worked at the bank and was clad in a J. C. Penney's business suit. She wasn't wearing lipstick. But Sarah imagined if she were, it wouldn't have been able to detract attention from the nickel-sized cluster of warts on her chin. She reminded Sarah of a warthog.

"Isn't he cute, Rhonda?" Warthog Lady asked Pumpkin Lady.

"Sure is," Pumpkin Lady said, licking some of the lipstick off of her lips and tapping her cubic zirconium wedding ring on the bar.

"Looks like you're married though," James said, eyeing Pumpkin lady's ring finger. "Too bad for me."

"I'm not," Warthog butted in.

"I'm taken, ladies," James said, pulling Alison toward him and throwing an arm over her shoulder. He always did that. *Why couldn't Alison see how much he adored her?* Alison smiled up at James.

"I see we have the same taste," a pasty man at the bar said. He didn't work at the bank. He was wearing the type of muscle shirt that you make yourself by cutting the side of a shirt with scissors all the way from the sleeve to the bottom of the shirt so that when you lean forward, people sitting on either side of you can see your entire bare stomach. This man's stomach, which was large, round, and white, should not have been shown off. He nodded arrogantly toward Alison. "I like mine with a few bruises too." Then he laughed and held up his beer.

Sarah clenched her jaw as she watched Alison's reaction.

"Booooo," Alison said. "You're a fucking dick." She stuck out her tongue at Muscle Shirt, slid out from under James's arm, and left his side. Her eyes were welling up as she brushed past Sarah.

"Be careful, buddy. If you say any shit like that again, I'll ask you to go."

"You can't ask me to go. I'm a paying customer."

"Just be respectful, all right?" James said calmly.

Sarah knew he was trying to avoid a confrontation. *But Jesus, some people just need to get smacked.* Her nostrils and her defenses were flaring. She looked over at Alison, who looked hurt but was not crying. She had begun washing pint glasses in the sink and was softly singing the "Strap your hands cross my engines" part from "Born to Run." Alison had always been rubber, and everyone else had always been glue. The very worst of insults never even ruffled her feathers. But today things were different. Things seemed to be hitting her harder and faster. *She needs you more than you need to smack that guy*, Sarah told herself as she joined Alison at the sink. They sang together as Alison washed and Sarah dried.

"You need anything, James?" Alison called.

"You want to see if I've got any food in the window?"

"Sure, dude," Alison said and headed toward the kitchen.

"Is she coming back?" Muscle Shirt asked James.

"What's it to you?" Sarah snapped.

"I wanna see if she likes it as rough as it looks like she does," he said, chuckling as he put his beer bottle to his mouth.

"That's it," Sarah said, sprinting toward him and pulling the beer out from his hands. He was just about to take a drink. So the top of the bottle was in his open mouth. It hit his tooth with a loud click as she yanked it away. "You need to go."

"You ain't the bartender, lady. 'Sides I paid for that beer," he countered, snatching it back from her. "It ain't a crime to talk." He started to pull his beer back up to his face. She snatched it back. He spilled it all over the front of his muscle shirt, pulling it back. Or maybe she spilled it all over the front of his muscle shirt as she yanked it back again. Perhaps it was a little bit of both.

"Jesus Christ, bitch, you wanna look like that girl who was just behind the bar with you or what?"

James tried to get Sarah by the back of the shirt but wasn't fast enough. She was already halfway over the bar, her hand in a ball. Her knuckles hit Muscle Shirt square in the nose. He leaped up, a bit discombobulated and tried to swing back at her. James wedged in between the two of them. He grabbed the man's balled-up fist and turned it. "Get out," he said to Muscle Shirt. "Get the fuck out now."

"She hit *me*, asshole," he said, waving his hands all over the place. "She spilled on me. And then she hit me."

"*You* spilled on yourself. And that's my sister, you piece of trash.

Go home and put on some clothes before everyone starts throwing up!" Sarah screamed, trying to get loose from James's grasp.

"I said get out!" James yelled at the guy. "Or I'll put you out!"

"That bitch is crazy!" Muscle Shirt yelled back. He was using one of those tiny bar napkins to wipe the blood spilling from his nose. "I'm going to get her fired from this place! You're not going to have a job when you wake up in the morning. You hear me!" He was leaving. But he was yelling all the while. Sarah could see the blood seeping through the napkins. A sense of satisfaction washed over her body like a waterfall.

Luke rushed from the back of the restaurant to the bar. James turned toward Sarah and put his hands on her shoulders. "Breathe," he told her. "It's okay. Breathe."

Sarah inhaled and exhaled and inhaled and exhaled. The bar was silent. Alison emerged from the kitchen with a tray full of food.

"Okay, who had the jalapeño poppers?" she asked, smiling. She held out the basket to the crowd around the bar.

"Um, I did," a guy on one of the stools said timidly, raising his hand.

"Okay, here you go. Those are so good. You are going to like those," she commented as she handed him the poppers. "And who had potato skins?" She handed the basket to another guy who raised his hand. "These are good too. I get them without the bacon 'cause I'm not a murderer. But really it's your prerogative." She shrugged her shoulders. "Working here, I guess makes me an accomplice anyway. So you need sour cream or anything, sir?"

"No, thank you, miss."

Nothing brings out the politeness in a bar crowd like one waitress who reaches over the bar to sock a guy in the nose and the waitress she was defending, who emerges from the kitchen none the wiser to hand out jalapeño poppers and potato skins.

****

At karaoke each week, there were always five or six Dolly Partons. There was a chunky blonde Dolly Parton who got a Reebok caught in the microphone cord, tripped, and spilled beer down the front of her shirt when she got off the stage. There was a sun-burned, red-haired Dolly Parton, wearing jean shorts over a one-piece swimsuit, who smoked in between verses of "I Will Always Love You." There was a Dolly in a matching yellow suit and jacket, who didn't know any of the words to "Nine to Five" and didn't bother to read them off of the teleprompter. There were several other Dollys, who all knew each other and clapped and yelled for one another.

Every table in the restaurant was occupied. There was no time to do anything else but take orders and bring out the food. If someone needed a refill, it was too bad. If someone needed something extra or something special, that was also too bad. And so sad. It was standing room only at the bar. And the kitchen was going down in flames, but not literally.

Sarah was too busy to stop, but she did anyway. She was watching the wonder that was Alison, who had pitchers of water and beer in her hands. In the middle of refilling someone's beverage, she yelled, "Anyone who needs something, put your left hand in and shake it all about!" Several hands set down their beers or forks or menus and sprang into sight to wave at Alison. They waved at Alison's smile, quirky brilliance, and ability to make them forget they had been waiting for whatever they were waiting for probably way too long. She quickly began checking in with all the customers now involved in the Hokey Pokey. Sarah began laughing when Alison shook her head at someone and told him, "I said left hand, sir." The man blushed and put his drink in his right hand. Then he shook his left hand back and forth at her as the redness left his cheeks. "There you go," she said, nodding her head in a gracious approval. "What can I get for you?"

"Just the check please."

"That's what it's all about!" she exclaimed.

There was a lady frantically shaking her left hand at Sarah.

Sarah walked toward her.

"What can I get for you, ma'am?"

"I asked for no cheese on this sandwich," she said, pointing at the cheese on her sandwich.

"Oh, well … we're not doing that today," Sarah said, shaking her head. Not quite as funny as Alison but funny enough, she thought. She turned around before an argument ensued and walked toward another table as fast as she could.

"What the hell am ..." Sarah heard the lady start to say. But she was long gone, already at another table, asking if they were ready to order. Her new table explained that they were ready and had been ready for a long time, that they needed their food extra fast because they were trying to catch a movie.

Sarah nodded. "Fast food," she commented.

"That's right," one lady said, handing Sarah her menu.

"Sort of like McDonald's," Sarah added.

"That's right," the lady said.

"Okay, do you want a Big Mac or Chicken McNuggets?"

The lady sitting next to her laughed. But she did not.

"I'll have fish and chips," she said with tightened lips.

Sarah was tempted. But she did not ask if the lady wanted them super-sized. Her friend ordered a small salad with a side of onion rings and a half-assed apology, which was just enough to dissuade Sarah from putting a pubic hair in the other lady's tartar sauce.

Lucky for Fish-and-Chips Lady and everyone else who told Sarah they were in a hurry, Big Joe and Little Joe were having a contest to see who could make what faster. Sarah's fish and chips were ready in six minutes.

Trisha was frantically digging in her apron as she came up to Sarah and asked, "What's twenty-five dollars minus seventeen dollars and sixty-two cents?"

"Seven dollars and thirty-eight cents."

"What?" she said, putting her hand around her good ear. "I lost my calculator. What's twenty-five dollars minus seventeen dollars and sixty-two cents?"

Several of the customers started laughing. Trisha turned red.

"She's just kidding," Sarah said loudly so that Trisha could hear her. "She knows its seven dollars and thirty-eight cents."

Trisha smiled. "Yep. I am a joker. That's what my husband always says. Doesn't Buster say that sometimes?" Trisha called to James.

"Yes, Trisha," James said, smiling.

Sarah could tell he was searching for something to say to Trisha, something that signified that he didn't care what she did or did not know or that he could sympathize with being embarrassed or hurt. But the words wouldn't arrange themselves in the correct order. So what he said instead was, "Forty-four," which Sarah guessed was the number of songs that had been karaokeed.

Trisha looked back at him. "Sarah told me seven thirty-eight," she said, panicky.

"It is seven thirty-eight, Trisha," he explained. "Forty-four is the number of hamburgers I've served today."

The people at the bar laughed again. Sarah was just about to give James a drink order for one of her tables but noticed two men sharing chicken wings who were still laughing at her friend.

"You hear about the *E. coli* they found in chicken on the news today?" she said loud enough to stop their laughter. "We are supposed to go ahead and serve what we have. But tomorrow we have to throw the rest out."

The men looked at each other's buffalo-sauce-covered faces and then at Sarah.

"You guys should probably drink some water," Sarah said to them.

James winked at her, shrugged, and gave them a couple of waters. Trisha asked Sarah if she thought the people at the bar were laughing at her because she was stupid.

"You are not stupid, sweetheart," Sarah told her. "No one knows everything."

"Yeah," she said, putting her head down a little lower. "But most people know how to do subtraction."

Sarah bit her lip. "Most but not all," she said, putting an arm around Trisha. "If you don't ask questions, you will never know the answers." Then Sarah told her, "If you feel like it is a dumb question, which I am sure it isn't, but if you *feel* like it is, next time, whisper it to me."

"Thanks, Sarah," she said with a smile so large that her cheeks looked like they had been stuffed with cotton balls.

Sarah leaned over the bar to get James's attention. He was fidgeting with a dish towel and reorganizing the liquor shelf in between taking customers' orders.

"Hey, put your boobs on this side," an overweight guy with a mustache yelled from the other side of the bar.

"No," James said to Sarah, trying to grab her arm. But he missed. Sarah walked over to the other side of the bar toward the guy with the mustache. James looked as if he were doing an inventory of his surroundings. He was tapping his foot and mumbling numbers under his breath. When Sarah approached the man with the mustache, she looked at the glass in his hand. "Is that a Diet Coke," she asked.

"No. It's—"

"Well, it should be," she said, cutting him off. "You know we have a maximum capacity in here. And every time you come in, you take up the space of four customers," she continued. "So you really shouldn't come in during happy hour because we lose business." She looked directly at him. Then she looked around the bar, which was rolling with laughter. She figured there were enough people around that he wouldn't try anything. He looked like he was searching for a comeback when James threw a glass on the ground and broke it.

"Slippery," he announced, keeping his eye on Sarah and the man with the mustache as she walked away.

"You need your tab, buddy?" he said.

"Yeah, I'll take it. Tell that lady to—"

"Leave it alone, Ben," someone yelled. "She was just having fun with you."

Mustache shut up, paid, and left.

"Alison is upset," Luke whispered into Sarah's ear.

"What's wrong with her?"

"I don't know. She was crying. She went into the bathroom."

Sarah already had a pretty good guess what was wrong with Alison. She had seen him. Their father, that son of a bitch, had crept in here of all places, to upset her, Sarah thought on her way to the bathroom.

When she entered the bathroom, Alison was crying in front of the mirror.

"I thought I saw him. I *really* thought I saw him again," she said through a wet layer of snot escaping the cavities in her nose and running toward her lips. Her face was more pale than red. After all, their father was a ghost, not a demon. "I went outside for a smoke, and I thought I saw him in our old car across the lot by the stop sign. I ran over there. But he drove off."

"But it wasn't him," Sarah told her.

Alison put her hands over her face and screamed into them. "God, one of these times, I really want it to be him. I know you've hated him since the day he disappeared, Sarah. But for me, he never disappeared. I see him all the time. It used to make me sad. Like, poor Dad, you know, kidnapped or lost or whatever, trying to make his way back to his family. You know it's possible he didn't run away from us ..." She put her hand on Sarah's shoulder. "But not real fucking probable. I'm not an idiot. I know everyone thinks I'm an idiot. But I'm not. I'm just hopeful. Or I was. Why couldn't he have said good-bye to me? I fucking miss him, and I just want a good-bye!"

"Byes are never good, remember?" Sarah said.

"Oh, Sarah, I just want to know it wasn't me. That's what I'm trying to fucking say. I just want to know it wasn't fucking *me*, you know what I mean?"

"It wasn't you," Sarah said, looking her right in the eyes.

Alison heaved a heavy sigh, like the air in her lungs weighed a ton. She gave half a smile and wiped the tears off of her face. But as she looked at Sarah, her eyes began to well up again. Sarah pulled her toward her body, just like she had done the other night. She could feel Alison's hot, salty tears running down her neck.

Ever since her dad left, all Sarah had ever wanted to do was hurt him, especially at moments like these. *Look at Alison. Look at what he's done to her. How could he do this to her?* She kept her sister in her arms until she could think of more things she loved about her dad than hated. He used to carry her around on his shoulders when she was little. It made her feel like she was a million feet tall. He let her pretend to drive the car, setting her on his lap and letting her steer the wheel in the driveway. He always waved longer than anyone else. He used to sing a song to her when she had bad dreams until she fell back to sleep. "We'd go down to the river. And into the river we'd dive ..." Sarah sang what she remembered of this song in Alison's ear. It was their dad who passed his love of Bruce Springsteen on to Alison and Sarah. They inherited it like a gene. In Alison, though, it was most prominent. For a minute, while Sarah was singing, she did forget how much she hated her dad. But when she finished singing, she remembered again.

Sarah figured that for Alison, seeing her dad was like the way people thought they heard the phone ring when they got into the shower. If you are expecting a call, the paranoia is ten times worse. But five years of jumping in and out of the shower had to make you start to wonder if you weren't mental. Plus, it greatly increased your chances of slipping and falling.

"I'm okay. I freaked out. But I am all right," she said into Sarah's ear.

"You sure?" Sarah asked wearily.

"Yeah, I mean, I will probably see him again in a couple of days anyway, right? Besides, Luke and Trisha are probably completely overwhelmed. Let's get out there." She looked at herself in the mirror. There was no mascara to run away, no eye shadow to congregate in the hinges of her eyelids. She waited for the color to return to her flesh and pulled Sarah out of the bathroom with her.

Alison was right. Luke was running around with a million drinks and plates of food all piled up on a tray, looking a bit like a child lost in the mall on Christmas. Trisha looked worse than a child lost in the mall on Christmas. She looked like the mother of a child lost in the mall on Christmas.

"What do you need?" Alison and Sarah asked Luke at the same time.

He pulled drinks off the tray and handed them to Alison. "These go to the jerk-offs at table twenty-six. I am not going back there." Then he pulled two baskets of wings off of the tray and handed them to Sarah. "Thirty-eight and thirty-nine," he said. Then he asked, "Is everybody okay?" He looked from Alison's face to Sarah's and then back to Alison's, then back to Sarah's.

They both nodded.

Alison put a tray of drinks on her head and walked slowly toward her table. She put her arm up, indicating a right turn. Then she turned left.

"Isn't that a left turn signal?" James asked Luke and Sarah.

They both shrugged.

"Don't have a car," Sarah answered.

"Never had a blinker go out," Luke said.

"Who cares?" a guy sitting at the bar added. *And he was right, to say the least.*

"Help!" Trisha called loudly from behind the swinging door to the kitchen. Sarah ran into the kitchen where Trisha was trying to put at least nine plates on a tray and pick it up. Sarah took some of the plates off, put them on another tray, and followed Trisha.

"Thank you," Trisha said over her shoulder at Sarah.

"You bet."

"Ali okay?"

"You better quit turning around and watch where you're going with that tray," Sarah said to Trisha, who was just about to run into a customer.

Trisha turned her face from back over her shoulder just before she almost crashed into a lady clapping her hands and swinging her hips to the music. The lady did not notice the near burger disaster. But Trisha paused for a stunned moment, gathered her momentum, and started walking again.

When everyone's tables seemed to be happy for the time being, the staff met in the kitchen.

"Order up," Luke said, sweeping Sarah up in his arms and throwing her tired body on top of the pickup window. Alison laughed hysterically, throwing herself onto the floor and slapping her palms on her kneecaps. Sarah fell off of the counter onto Alison. Luke tried to catch Sarah and fell on top of the both of them. They all ended up in a heap on the floor.

Trisha was laughing so hard that tears squeezed themselves right out of her eyes and slid down her chubby cheeks. She watched as they all climbed off of one another. Just as they were getting up, she yelled, "Dog pile!" and plopped her pudgy body right on top of them in mid-stance. They went crashing to the sticky kitchen floor again and gasped for air from under her flabby dolphin-shaped frame. *I don't know how many definitions there are for family*, Sarah thought as she grunted through a dog pile of smashed laughter, but she was sure this was in there somewhere.

It was a rare occasion when Doug did not come in to check up on his employees at least once a day. But by the end of the dinner rush, Doug had not shown his fat face. The energy and happiness of his employees was contagious. It felt like a carnival. At seven in the evening, the waitstaff began drinking Bloody Marys—even Trisha. When the crowds went home, they closed early. Sarah walked home with Luke and Trisha because James had asked her if he could take Alison out after work. "That way, she doesn't have to be a part of whatever the Joes are planning to do to Anthony."

Three Cherries

CHAPTER 11

James would take any given weeknight
in any given bar—
when they laughed until they choked,
drank until they were broke,
like every third bar stool,
because even as kids
Alison was the best person
to get rained on with,
the best person to get blamed on with
for things they didn't do
but had both thought of
separately
at the same time:
one,
two,
three,
let's jump
in the car.
He would pay while she pumped.
She could drive, and he could ride—
if he could just get her to open up,
he would crawl inside
her heart,
sew it back together,
and stay there forever.

"You tell me six years ago I be crap-shootin' with a pork rind, I'da been laughin' in all my mug shots," Buster told Bob, who was resting on a bar stool in front of him.

"Well, if you would have told me or Josie," Bob said, resting a callused hand on his wife's tanned thigh, "we'd have met a true success story like you … I mean that's the way the system is supposed to work; you turned into such an upstanding citizen …" Bob looked at Josie, who nodded her head for him to continue, even though he was getting somewhat emotional.

"He's gonna cry," Josie interjected.

"Aw, success ain't a tearjerker, pork chop. It's a helping hand from the J-man. That's all." He patted Bob on the arm. "Now I got the tickets. But I ain't got the green. Henry told me to tell ya he'd come up to the station tomorrow and give you the Benjamins." Buster stopped suddenly and shouted across the bar, "It ain't a mailbox! You two come sit down at the bar and play your tic-tac-toe!"

Terrence and Jennifer stopped shoving napkins into the jukebox and guiltily walked over to the bar. They sat down in front of Buster and next to Bob and Josie.

"You really shouldn't bring your kids to the bar," Bob said, shaking his head back and forth.

"Shit, Bob. I ain't givin' 'em booze. They're drinking from Sherly's temple. You see all them cherries floatin' around?" Buster said, tapping on the side of the beer mug sitting in front of Jennifer. "'Sides these cats …" He made a sweeping motion to all the customers sitting at the bar. "… spoil the soda crackers outta these kids."

Terrence and Jennifer both smiled, showing their cherry-colored teeth. Buster handed Terrence a pen and a bar napkin to play tic-tac-toe on with his sister.

"Like I said, here's the tickets." Buster handed Bob an envelope with thirty-three counterfeit scratch tickets inside. Bob gave the envelope to Josie, who looked inside and then gave it back to Bob.

"It's David's money, you know. There's no crime in giving a man's money to his kids," Josie assured Buster. "You're not a criminal anymore."

"I know." Buster nodded. Then he put a hand around the side of his mouth and lowered his voice as he said, "But watch what you say about Pops in front of the popsicles, Mrs. Pork Chop. These kids don't need no reminders of my checkerboard past … if you catch my dirty driftwood."

Bob and Josie both nodded.

"We'd better go," Bob told Buster as he noticed Alison and James walk into the bar.

"Hey there," Bob told Alison as he passed her on their way out.

Alison smiled. "Hey, Bob. Hi, Josie. You guys just hang out and drink beers all day or what?"

Josie let out a nervous laugh.

"Something like that," Bob said, grabbed ahold of Josie's hand, and led her out the door.

****

Jerry's was the only bar in Jasper County, not counting Doug's restaurant. It was the bar that Buster worked at four nights a week. It was also the bar that Charles spent the last ten years of his life in. It wasn't far from Doug's, about six cigarettes away, by Alison's measurements. It sat like a house on the corner of Pine and Ninth with a long driveway for parking. It was house-shaped and house-colored. It had a regular house door and doorbell. This was because Jerry had turned his home into a bar. Well, he had turned his basement into a bar. You had to walk through his front hallway, past his and his wife's shoes scattered about the "All of God's creatures are welcome here" matt, and Jerry's coat closet, which was always wide open to show off all of Jerry's camouflage coats and hats and the fancy boots that you wear in the water when you hunt things that you hunt in the water. But Jerry had the liquor license and paid taxes and everything. So it was a bar. And it was a house.

Inside Jerry's bar, the walls were covered with stuffed dead animals, beady-eyed little squirrels, prairie dogs in mid-prance, foxes, ducks, and other birds that looked like ducks but were probably something else. There was one sad little glassy-eyed stuffed deer in the corner where the unisex bathroom was located. It was a funny place for the deer to stand, as if it was there to tell you that there was someone already using the restroom or watch the door for you while you were using the restroom or bash through the restroom door with its angry dead antlers while you were in mid–tampon insertion. That last one was what Alison claimed its purpose was. So she did not use the bathroom when she went to this bar. She went outside. Jerry's always gave Alison the creeps. She said that the animals whispered, "Killer, killer, killer," in her ear.

"Hunting is a sport, like tennis or anything else," Sarah had tried to tell her.

"Yeah, except in tennis, the bullets are fuzzy green balls that playfully *bounce* instead of brutally *murder*," she responded.

"There are risks in every sport," Sarah tried. Then she added, "Tennis balls aren't playful. They go really fast. Actually, you *could* get seriously hurt if you got hit with a tennis ball."

"Tennis balls don't get lodged in your lungs and explode gunpowder," Alison said. But just like working in the restaurant, carrying around dead chickens and cows all day long, Jerry's was an inevitable part of Alison's life. She apologized as she passed each stuffed animal but made do because it was the only other bar in town and a girl had to go out every once in a while no matter how much she loved all of God's creatures.

****

James knew that when he dragged Alison to Jerry's after work, he would have to be careful what he said to her.

Jerry and his wife had painted a mural on the wall not so realistically depicting the flatlands and sunset. There were little hunters scattered about the field with their whiskey-red cheeks and noses, their rifles on their shoulders. They must have had to paint a field because their artistic ability would have limited them from painting an actual forest. It had never really made any sense to James. But then again, he didn't really know anything about hunting. The bar stools were tree trunks. And the tables were tree trunks with glass over them, which seemed like another inconsistency to him. But maybe it was a little hunting joke or story that he didn't know about. And if you were a hunter, maybe you were laughing out loud, remembering the fields with deer running through them and the glass tree-trunk story.

James and Alison sat down on a couple of lacquered tree stumps across from Buster, who was in the middle of telling a customer about the J-man saving his soul back in '89 just before he made parole. "One cat was locked up thirty-somethin' years and happy as pie. Every day I saw him in the grub room, talking about 'Jesus this' and 'God that.' I said to myself, 'I gotta have a shit shoot with this dude.' He gave me a Bible and—" Buster stopped, midstory. "Oh, hey, cats!" He waved at Alison and James. "Rest yer dogs. I'll be right back," he told the customer.

"Hi, Buster," Alison said. "How's business?"

"Slow as Gramma Moses," he answered slowly as he surveyed the scrapes on her face.

"I'm fine. The Joes are taking care of it," she explained.

He nodded, setting two bottles of MGD in front of them.

"I think we must have snatched up your customers. You know everyone goes to Doug's for karaoke. We were busy as hell," James said, changing the subject.

"Aww, I don't mind it. I like having the time to chat with these cats. You guys know how I like shit-shooting." He made a gun with his pointer finger and thumb and fired an air bullet at James.

"Yeah, Bus, we know," James said.

"Got a new tat," Buster said, proudly pointing to a bandage on his shoulder.

"Didn't think you had any room," Alison said, laughing.

"There's always room for the J-man," he said, peeling down the gauze to reveal the face of a cartoon-colored Jesus Christ. Directly above Jesus, there was a pirate holding a snake, and directly below Jesus, there was a sort of mermaid hooker.

"Why'd you put him above the naked lady?" Alison asked.

"Well, I just told Tess to put it wherever the hell she could find a clean piece a' skin." Tess was Jerry's wife, who also worked in the bar as both a bartender and a tattoo artist. "She picked this shoulder right here," Buster said, pulling the bandage back up and pressing it firmly against his bulging bicep. "It ain't too bad a spot though, right? Plus, I'm gonna like looking at the J-man when I'm lifting barbells. It'll be like, if this cat can carry a cross, I oughta be able to raise a few hundred pounds of metal, right?" He laughed. "Make sure you tell her you like it. You know how people like to hear compliments," he said nodding his head up and down at James and Alison. Then he threw a soft, meaty left hook into the side of Alison's arm.

"Ouch, Buster. I weigh half of what you do, remember?"

"Sorry, Pussy Cat Doll!" he shouted. "I forgot!" He leaned over and rubbed the place he had punched. "I'm really sorry," he said again with an apologetic look on his face. He leaned over farther and kissed Alison's arm. "Better?"

"Not really," she said after an uncomfortable laugh and a sip of beer.

He shrugged. "Works with my sugar-bunny ... Gotta get back to the gig," Buster said and walked over to a new customer. As he did, he called, "Put that cold beer bottle on it if it still hurts after a while!"

"Did he hit you hard?" James asked, concerned. He wondered if Alison's arms looked like her face, scraped and bruised.

"Yeah," Alison said, laughing. "I know he didn't mean to. But he's like 250 pounds of pure muscle. Crap," she said, rubbing her arm again. "I just got punched by Jesus."

James chuckled as he fiddled with the plastic on his box of cigarettes.

"If Jesus were an ex-con."

"Yeah, but Buster didn't hurt anybody. He went to jail for making fake documents or something."

"Oh yeah. That's right. Social Security cards," James agreed, nodding his head. "Luke told me Trisha said he wasn't making enough money at the Kinko's in town, so he sort of promoted himself," he added.

"That's one way to look at it," Alison said, putting her hand on top of James's to get him to stop fidgeting.

"You know ..." he said, beginning to bounce his right leg up and down to make up for not being able to move his hand. He was always fidgeting. When he stopped moving, the numbers in his head fought with one another. They spit and kicked and spun. Moving was the only way to make them sit still. "I used to think Luke and Trisha would get married," James said.

Alison gave James a confused look.

"I mean, I know Luke's gay," James explained. "But those two are really tight."

"They are, aren't they? Well, the only difference between marriage and friendship is sex, I guess."

"Oh, they had sex, remember," James replied.

"That's true ..." Alison said. She appeared to think for a minute. "Maybe there is no difference between friendship and marriage," she said hesitantly. Then she added, "I guess we are as good as married." James felt his cheeks warm.

"I'm glad we're here together, Ali. You needed to get your mind off of things for a while. How are you doing?" She looked sad for a minute. Then she smiled and said, "At this exact second, I am happy."

James smiled, both on the inside and the outside. It felt good to see her like this.

****

Alison studied James's eyes. James had beautiful blue eyes. They were sea-to-shining-sea-blue eyes. Sweet-irises-of-liberty-blue eyes. And they were the bank and trust of his face, changing and cashing in the value of each word spoken. James paid such close attention to Alison when she talked that she felt as though each syllable that came out of her mouth was of the utmost importance to him. He was watching only her, his friend, his protagonist, his clandestine love. Alison cared for James, but she wasn't quite sure how to love him the way she knew that he loved her. She reached for her box of cigarettes that *had been* just sitting on the bar by her beer.

"Where are my cigarettes?" she asked, looking along the edge of the bar.

James's face lit up, and his eyes began to laugh before there was the actual sound of laughing. She followed his eyes across the bar to a little boy just tall enough to fit his chin on the bar. Terrence had drawn a mustache on his upper lip with a magic marker. He was studying Alison's box of cigarettes, opening and closing it.

"Hey, buddy, where did you come from?" Alison asked.

"America," Terrence answered with a sheepish grin.

"What are you doing here, Terrence?" James asked.

Terrence shrugged and began to dump the cigarettes from the box out onto the countertop of the bar.

"Hey, can I have one of those?" Alison asked him.

"One dower pwease," he said, holding out his hand.

She pulled an imaginary dollar from her pocket and handed it to him. He handed her a cigarette. Tess spotted the child in the middle of talking to a customer at the bar. She told the customer to hang on a second and made her way toward him.

"I'm sorry," she said to Alison and James. "Buster, you need to be keeping an eye on your kids here!" she yelled in a cigarette-scratched voice. She pried the box of cigarettes from Terrence's hand and scooted its evicted tenants toward James and Alison. Then she handed Alison the empty box. Terrence began to cry.

"Terrence, don't act like a baby. You are in a bar," she scolded. "Go ask yer stepdaddy for a freakin' Coke or something."

Before Alison could tell her she had tattooed a rather impressive Woody-the-Woodpecker-style Jesus Christ on Buster's shoulder, Tess turned and walked away. Buster came over to Terrence and picked him up.

"Sorry, guys. Is Terry botherin' you?"

"No, Bus," Alison said, wondering why Buster was always bringing his kids to work instead of leaving them with Luke or Trisha. But Buster answered her question without her having to ask.

"This place is like an amusement park to these kids. They have a real blast drinking sodas and playing games. Plus, I get to spend time with them. So if he's botherin' or my little catwoman's botherin', just give me the say-so."

Alison surveyed the bar to see if she could spot Jennifer crawling around on the floor somewhere. James nudged Alison and pointed to the stuffed deer by the bathroom. There Jennifer stood on her tiptoes, putting peanuts in its dead stuffed mouth.

"They're fine. They're family. We can keep an eye on them," James told Buster.

Terrence wiggled out of Buster's arms and went up to Alison and James. He took hold of the edge of the bar and rested his chin on it in front of them. His marker mustache stretched into a smile.

"Have a beer then, on Buster!" Tess called as she walked over to James and Alison and handed them both another beer. Then she took a couple of dollars out of Buster's tip jar and put them in the register.

"Hi," Terrence said and waved a tiny hand over the bar in front of James and Alison.

"Hi," Alison said, putting her chin down on the bar so it was level with his. James did the same. The little boy was smiling so big that the ends of his marker mustache touched the sides of his nose. Terrence took a peanut from their bowl and held it out to James. James reached for it, and Terrence pulled it back.

"One dowar, pwease."

James gave Terrence an imaginary dollar. Terrence handed him the peanut and shouted, "Oooo, kissy, kissy!" He pointed upward toward a duck suspended from the ceiling with a piece of mistletoe that had been dangling from its bill since last Christmas.

"It's not Christmas yet, Terrence," Alison explained.

But the six-year-old was adamant.

"Kissy! Kissy! *Kissy!*"

"I need to bring Terrence with me on dates," James said, laughing.

"Yeah, you—" Alison started.

"*Kissy*," Terrence interrupted.

"Whatever." Alison shrugged and kissed James. She meant it to be quick enough to satisfy Terrence and light enough so that she and James could go back to their conversation. It was a kiss, at first, just as Alison expected—forced but friendly—except James touched her on the side of the face, his pinky under her chin. And she meant to touch his knee, but his other hand was on his knee and their fingers interlocked so gently that she began to forget they were touching. Her stomach was, all of a sudden, void like in the middle of a dive off of the high board at the water park. The only thought running though her head was *Touch me. Touch me. Touch me.* It ran back and forth and back and down the steps of her spine. It ran circles around her rib cage. Then it grabbed on to her heart and snagged it right down the middle. It ran through her so fast that none of her other thoughts could catch up to it.

There was a rush that started from inside of her body and worked itself out through her cheeks so that they were warm. On her left and his right, their eyelashes brushed up against one another like two beach combs. She couldn't think of anything else except his warm tongue on top of hers, not doing much of anything, just gently touching like their hands, interlocking. When it was over, they rested their foreheads on one another's, forming a triangle that framed a six-year-old boy's face, in a bar, in America.

The only thing Alison could think to do was put her head on James's shoulder. She had done it a hundred times. But this time, it was different. The two had a connection. There was static between his collar and her cheekbone. And she felt like a sock clinging there as the two of them tumbled from a big Laundromat dryer into some stranger's plastic basket.

"Why do you like me?" Alison asked, her head still on his shoulder.

"What do you mean?" he asked.

"You know what I mean, James. I'm a little used. I'm not apologizing ... I am the way I am. I just ..." Her voice trailed off, and she turned to the side to watch her words run away. When she turned back around, she said, "My dad would be disappointed."

His face looked sad when he softly put his hands on the sides of hers and said, "You are not a disappointment. You are kind and fierce and brave. You are the thing I look forward to every day."

"Thank you."

"I would get rid of every number in my head to have your talent."

The bar was noisy. People were talking loudly over one another as well as the music. But Alison couldn't have been more focused on James's words. Maybe it was because they were so flattering. Maybe it was because his voice was so calm. Maybe it was because she had a strange sensation in her hands and feet, like she had been sitting on them for a long time and she couldn't figure out how to make them feel normal again. There was also a feeling inside her stomach. It was a cross between getting punched hard and getting kissed lightly.

"Oh yeah? What's my fucking talent?"

"You are a poet. You can make someone fall in love with you just by talking to you. You make everyone smile. I wish I could make people feel the way you do. I would throw out all the numbers in my head. Being able to count and remember what it is you counted isn't a talent."

"Neither is talking. But I'll take it."

"It's not just talking. You are able to put things into words that make people feel how you do. And everyone should feel things as deeply as you do. Remember when we were little and you used to tell me stories?"

Alison nodded.

"You told me a story one time about a boy like me who had so many numbers in his head that there was no room for words. So the boy never talked. But one day an angel came to him and told him that there weren't any words in his head because they were all in his heart. And the boy started talking and the words that came out of his mouth made everyone in the town love him so much they started bringing him all the most beautiful things they could think of, like paintings and flowers and gold. They thought he was the only one who could appreciate beautiful things because he was the only one who used words beautiful enough to explain them. But he was sad because he was given everything that was beautiful and there was nothing left for anyone else to look at. And he gave everything back. He told the people who had given these things to him that beautiful things didn't need explaining."

"I kind of remember that story," Alison said. "I think it was a poem I wrote while my mom was driving Sarah and me somewhere. I wrote it with a crayon on the back of a box of animal crackers. I think I just changed it into a story for you."

"Well," he said, fidgeting with the label on his beer bottle and then looking up at her. "That story made me feel very good." He bit his lip. "I wish I could tell you how good it made me feel. I wish I could use the words in my heart sometimes like the boy in the story. But I don't know how." He looked down again and shuffled his feet back and forth on the stool.

"I can't *believe* you remember that story."

"I remember them all."

They were both quiet for a minute, and then James spoke. "You know this is the bar my dad used to come to," he said, catching Alison's eyes with his.

They blinked in unison.

"I know," she said. Then she added, "My dad came here too."

"Not like my dad. My dad's ghost is probably in here somewhere."

"I think …" Alison paused. "I think that your dad loved you," she said, which was not what she was thinking. What she was thinking was that James's father's ghost was definitely in there somewhere.

"No, he didn't, Alison," James said without pain in his words. "*Your* dad loved me." It was true; James was the son Alison's father never had, and her father was the dad James never had.

Both of them were avoiding eye contact, looking down at each other's feet. Hers were bare. They were resting on top of each other like a pair of hands in a senior photograph. Say, "Class of '94 rules!" Click. His were still in his sneakers, a pair of Reeboks that looked older than the deer watching the restroom. There was tension in the silence. James spoke first.

"I hated myself for hating my dad. But I *did* hate him. I really did. But then I didn't want anyone else to hate him because of me. I think I was afraid that cruelty was contagious. Or genetic. Maybe that's why I have forgiven him. I don't know how. I just did."

"Your dad was hard to like—love," she hurriedly corrected and then didn't know if she should have.

"No one loved my dad, Alison. They loved your dad. Your dad was the good one. Did you ever wonder why my mom and Luke and I were always staying over at your house all the time? It was because your dad came and got us. Every night when he came home from work, he looked in on us. Sometimes he came in and told us to come with him back to stay at your house. If your dad hadn't come in, I would have been dead sixteen times."

"I didn't know that my dad was the one who brought you to our house."

"I know."

"You know why your dad took care of me?"

"Because he loved you," she answered.

"Because he loved *you*," he answered back. "He knew that I loved you as much as he did."

She looked at James, who was looking at her, touching her knee with his hand.

"Shots!" she exclaimed, unable to know what to do with those words. "We'll take two shots of whiskey!" she called to Buster.

"Comeen wite up," Terrence called from behind the bar.

"I got it, sonny," Buster said, patting Terrence on the top of his head. "You go play with Jennifer." He poured two shots and set them in front of James and Alison.

They sat in silence again. Alison was no longer looking at James. But his eyes were burning cigar-sized holes through the skin on her left cheek. She could almost smell burning flesh.

"Your coaster's on fire," James said, pointing to the bar top with his eyes.

"What?" She looked down at the cherry that had somehow managed to parachute from her cigarette onto a highlife coaster. "You are," she said, pouring some of her beer onto the coaster.

He was uncomfortably playing with the label on his beer bottle, pulling the edges loose and then pressing them back down. "I really loved your dad."

"I really loved my dad too," Alison said. "My dad *was* a good one," she admitted.

"He was the best."

"To my dad," she said. She put her shot up in the air. "We will never stop looking for you," she added.

"To your dad … wherever he may be," James said, touching his shot glass to hers. They both drank.

Out of the corner of one eye, Alison could see Terrence and Jennifer playing Communion in the corner of the bar with a bowl of peanuts.

Terrence was saying, "Body of Christ," and placing a peanut in Jennifer's folded hands.

"Meow," Jennifer said, putting the peanut in her mouth and doing the sign of the cross.

Terrence scolded her. "You have to say, 'Amen,' not 'Meow.' Okay? Let's do it again."

Alison smiled.

"Twenty-six," James said, almost in a whisper.

"What?"

"That's how many times I've seen you smile today."

"Really? That's a lot. I've smiled that much just today?"

"It's a lot less than usual." He paused and seemed to be trying to put more words together. The he looked at her and said, "I want to tell you something. And I want you to not interrupt, just listen. Okay?"

"Okay," Alison said skeptically.

"I don't think your dad is gone."

"*What?* What do—"

"I said hear me out. How many times have you guys won playing scratch tickets at the general store?"

"I don't know."

"I do. Anyway, it's rhetorical."

"Okay."

"It's not statistically possible. You've made, on average, two hundred bucks a month for the past five years. Have you ever thought about that?" Alison opened her mouth to comment, But he kept on talking. "Someone is hooking you guys up. Someone is taking care of you. And if it's not your dad, then who is it?"

"How is that possible?"

"I don't know, but ..." He stopped talking when Buster approached.

"Hey, don't stop, drop, and roll, 'cuz a' me. Saw you two doing a little spit swapping. 'Bout time."

James and Alison both blushed.

"You cats sharing a litter box tonight or what?"

"Buster," James said, giving him a *go away* look.

"All right, I'll leave you alone. But be careful," he said, eyeing James and pointing a large finger at Alison. "This kitty's got more punch than a high school prom."

Alison picked up a washrag from the bar and threw it at Buster.

But what did that kiss mean? Alison wondered. So many things were happening so fast, her brain couldn't keep up. What was once stashed away safely in a cocoon had come out as a butterfly. And as they walked home together, Alison tried to figure out how she would deal with that change. She had never had wings before.

****

Big Joe looked in the window as Little Joe knocked on Anthony's door. "Keep knocking. He's in there all right," he told Little Joe. "Oh, here he comes," Big Joe said, stepping back up on the porch next to Little Joe.

"Hi, Anthony Milano?" Little Joe asked.

"Yeah, who are you?" Anthony said, looking from Joe to Joe.

"Census takers. Is it just you, or you got roommates?" Little Joe asked as he tried to see around Anthony into his living room.

"Yeah, I got a roommate ... Isn't it a little late to be going door-to-door?"

"Yes, sir, Mr. Milano, long workday. Is your roommate home?" Big Joe asked, pushing past Anthony and walking into his living room where his roommate was playing a video game from the couch in only his underwear.

"Hey, I didn't invite you in!" Anthony called.

"He's just got to ask your roommate a few questions," Little Joe explained. "So you got a dog?" Big Joe heard Little Joe ask as he approached the guy on the couch.

"Okay, here's the deal, buddy. Your roommate did a real shitty thing to a real nice person who just happens to be a friend of mine."

The guy paused his game and looked up at Big Joe.

"Now you have a couple of options. You can sit here and watch us kick the shit out of him, or you can leave. But what you cannot do is jump in and start throwing punches, 'cause then you're going to get the shit kicked out of you too."

"Hey, man," the guy said as he grabbed a pair of pants from the arm of the couch and put them on. "Anthony and I aren't even that good of friends," he said, walking sideways toward the kitchen; then he ran out the back door.

Little Joe pushed Anthony away from the door and back into his house where Big Joe stood.

"You guys aren't census takers, are you?"

"Nope," Big Joe said and punched Anthony in the stomach. He grunted and bent down.

"We're friends with that girl you beat up the other day. Remember her?" Little Joe asked.

Anthony stood back up and shook his head. "No, I don't know her."

"Sure you do. Let me help you remember," Little Joe said and head-butted him.

Anthony went backward and landed on the coffee table. Big Joe picked him up and threw him into a wall. "You remember that sweet girl now?" he asked.

"Yes, but—" Little Joe grabbed him by the hair and slammed his head into the TV.

"Well, we think you might need someone to teach you how to treat women," Big Joe said, kicking Anthony's legs out from under him.

"Not the legs, Big Joe. Remember?"

"Oh, shit. Sorry."

"Just be careful," he said, pulling Anthony to his feet and holding his arms behind his back while Big Joe kicked him in the balls.

"Hey!" he exclaimed. "I think I got an idea for a friendly little competition. When he can't get back up, let's see who can break the most stuff in the house in under five minutes."

"Hey, good one!" Big Joe said, punching Anthony in the stomach.

"Hey!" Jean called from the porch were she was sitting with Linda, Luke, and Sarah as she saw Alison and James come walking up the driveway. "Come join the porch party."

Linda's eyes were staring blankly at a group of ants drinking from, or stuck in, a river of White Zinfandel recently spilled at the bottom of the porch steps. Bob's ears perked up when he saw Alison walk up the porch steps.

"Mom was just about to tell us about how Dad asked her to marry him," Sarah said.

"Really?" Alison asked as she and James sat down next to one another on top of the porch railing.

"He was holding my feet," she began.

"What?" James and Alison said at the same time.

Linda was quiet. Jean had told her this story before.

"We were in gym class. I was doing sit-ups. I was sweating like a pig. We were supposed to be able to do twenty-five to pass the fitness test. I wanted to give up at twenty. My stomach hurt so bad." She held her stomach, remembering the cramps. "I told your dad that I couldn't do it. He said I could. I said I couldn't, and we went back and forth like that. In the meantime, I had done two more. Mr. Puttman, the gym teacher, was watching me the whole time. That jerk didn't think I could do it either. But your dad did. He said, 'If you can do twenty-five, I'll marry you.'"

"Seriously?" Sarah asked.

Linda nodded her head up and down.

"Yes. And I did it. I handed in my fitness test and signed my name 'Mrs. Jean Robbins.' I've had that name for over half of my life."

There was a long silence that was too uncomfortable even for the bugs to break. Jean pictured a locust standing as still as a cardboard cutout in his own uncomfortable shell on the bark of a tree limb somewhere in her yard, waiting for someone, anyone but him, to say something.

"I am going to get more wine," Sarah said finally as she pushed herself up from the porch swing.

"Sit back down. I'll get it," Jean said, touching Sarah on the arm.

Sarah sat back down. Alison got up and sat on the porch swing next to her.

Jean listened to the conversation twirling in through the squares in the screen door with the breeze. The porch swing creaked as her two daughters began to rock with one another. She filled her plastic cup with wine and brought more plastic cups and the box with the remaining wine outside. She gave a cup to Alison and James and then filled their cups, along with everyone else's.

When Jean sat back down, Bob came and sat next to her. He rolled over, and Jean scratched him on the belly.

"Dad asked Mom to marry him in a high school gymnasium!" Alison exclaimed proudly.

"I heard," Luke said and smiled.

"A gymnasium proposal. How romantic!" Sarah said sarcastically. "At least he was kneeling," she added.

Bob hopped back up on the swing and snuggled in between Sarah and Alison.

"How did you get so cynical, Sarah?" Jean asked. "What your dad did in that gymnasium is show me what I was capable of. That moment was the first time I ever did something I didn't think I could do. After your dad told me I could do those stupid sit-ups, I did them. You know, you can do a lot of things you don't think you can. You just have to have someone else think you can. All you need is one person to tell you that you can do it. One person. Your dad, he was that one person, and now that he's gone, who do I—"

Sarah interrupted. "I'm not being cynical, Mom. There is literally nothing romantic about that story. Anyway, Dad left a long time ago, and you have been doing just fine without him."

"Who taught you two to interrupt everybody all the time? It had to have been your father."

"Actually—" Sarah started to say.

"Because it's very rude," Jean interrupted.

Alison, James, Luke, Linda, and Sarah laughed. Jean started to laugh too.

"Whoopsy," she said, setting down her glass of wine. Bob's eyes followed the plastic cup to the porch floor. But he did not move from his spot between Sarah and Alison.

"I know that things are different now than they were then … but you can do whatever the hell you want to. You've always been able to do whatever the hell you want. If there's something you don't think you can do, well then, try and do it at least nine hundred times and then," Sarah said, pointing her finger, "decide that you can't do it. Thinking and doing are like … are like … cats and dogs."

"Cats and fucking dogs," Alison agreed, smacking her sister on the arm and nodding her head up and down.

"Why do you have to say 'fuck' all the time, Ali?" Jean asked, taking a sip from her glass.

"I don't fucking know, Mom. Why aren't you trying to fucking find him?"

"He left us, shitmouth. Any man that could leave us, I don't want. Even if I did love him. I don't want that."

"I don't want that either," Alison said. "I guess I just miss him. Don't you fucking miss him? I mean when did you stop loving each other?" she asked, her eyes filling up with tears.

Jean felt Alison's question was a cruel one, dredging up bones that were buried but never eulogized. But she knew Alison wasn't trying to hurt her with it. Jean tilted her head and blinked her eyes. Bob mimicked her.

"I could never stop loving your father. But you have to remember I never even saw him. And I guess it's not him that I miss. What I miss is him finishing the crossword puzzle for me. I could never answer any of the worldly figures or foreign names, and he never could get the books or authors or vocabulary. Now that he's gone, all the answers to the things that he knew are blank in every crossword I do. I guess maybe half of the answers in his crossword are probably missing too."

"I can't figure out if that is really beautiful or really sad," Linda said as she looked at her friend.

"It's really sad. Symmetry is only beautiful when you are a butterfly," Alison said as one brave tear was the first to jump ship. James got up and stood behind Alison. He put a hand on her shoulder. She put a hand on his hand.

Jean watched their hands on top of one another as she continued to talk. "I miss the heat that came from his body next to mine in bed, him taking out the chicken from the freezer to thaw. I miss him filling up the gas in the car for me. I miss the way he folded towels." Jean had always folded the towels into rectangles, and David had always folded them into squares. David never showed Jean how to do it his way, and she never showed him how to do it her way. Five years after he'd been gone, there was still one towel in their bathroom closet neatly folded into a square that she had never been able to bring herself to use.

Jean paused, lit a cigarette, and took a drag. Then she added, "But I don't miss *him*. I barely even saw him in those last few years we were together. By the time I would have noticed he had gotten a haircut, it would have all grown back. I thought the man hadn't been to a barber in years."

"You don't miss *him*?" Alison questioned. Her face looked the way it looked during the credits of a movie where someone died, both tragically and unexpectedly right at the end. Jean half expected her to scream, "What a terrible ending!" But she didn't. She just sat there with her mouth wide open. But no words came out. It was open just for the sake of being open, Jean guessed.

"He loved you two," Jean said, looking at her daughters. "He loved all of us." Some leftover smoke escaped from Jean's lungs, and she muffled a cough with the side of her cup. She set it down and said, "He was a good man. The man I married was a good man. And I wouldn't change anything in my life, even if I could."

"I would like to know what made him give up. That's what I would like to know," Sarah said angrily.

"Me too," Jean said. "But I am afraid we don't get to know." She followed a squirrel with her eyes across her yard and into Henry and Pam's driveway. *I didn't know Buster had a motorcycle*, she thought.

****

Buster smiled across the kitchen table at his old friend. He and Fish had done time together and were the best of friends "on the inside." He had never seen him "on the outside." Fish was a con man at heart but loyal to his friends. He shook his head in disbelief. "I can't believe you're out, Fish. I sorta thought you had roots growing under your cot." He laughed. "I mean you're one fish I never thought could fly the coop."

"Me too!" Fish laughed. "But I did and I'm already putting a crew together. I got a real good business opportunity for you."

"Shit, Fish, unless you want me to help you make jigsaw puzzles outta toilet paper for the Hispanics so you can trade 'em for weed again, I'm afraid I can't do business with you. I'm a proud supporter of the J-man now. Got a bumper sticker and everythin'. I ain't makin' no waves but in the bathtub anymore. Been saved, married, and behaved. So be careful with them curses. If you wake up my wife with them, she'll beat your behind. And then she'll beat mine."

"For real, no illegal shit," Fish said, furrowing his brows as he took a swig of the beer Buster had given him almost as soon as he let him in the front door.

"Truth be to God," he said, nodding his head up and down. "But I won't preach about the J-man if you don't start pushin' anything that's gonna send the pigs snortin' at my door."

Fish laughed. He got up from the table with his beer and picked up a picture of Terrence and Jennifer from the ledge of the window above the kitchen sink. "These your kids?" he asked.

"One's mine. One's the neighbor's," Buster answered.

"Sorry, man," Fish said sympathetically.

"It ain't even a hand I gotta deal. He's as gay as the jack a' spades," Buster explained.

"This him, the one in the cowboy hat?" Fish asked, setting down the picture of Terrence and Jennifer and picking up a picture of Luke, Trisha, and Terrence.

"Right hand green," Buster said, walking over to Fish and high-fiving his right hand. "And that puffy little blonde is my bread and butter," he added. "She ain't the brightest crayon in the box. But she sure is the most colorful."

Fish didn't respond. He was looking intently at the picture.

"I think I met this guy," Fish said, pointing to the picture.

"Cool Hand Luke?"

"Yeah, I think his name was Luke. Works at a bar called Doug's …"

"Hell yeah he does! Small town, big coincidence."

"I gave him Milano's number. He was looking for someone."

Buster froze.

"You gave him Milano's number?"

"Yeah, he seemed sad. So did his friends. Milano ain't gonna kill him, just tell them where he is. If them kids tell him I asked, he will help find who they're looking for."

"Fraggle fuckin' Rock, Fish!" Buster said. "That's the wrong kinda help you're giving out for free."

"It's cool. Milano owes me. Remember? I gave him the Heimlich in the lunch room, saved his big old gangster ass from a little bitty hot dog. Plus if you need to find someone, he's your man."

"It's a sticky-tape situation," Buster said, walking back over to the table. He picked up his beer and took a swig that required three gulps. Buster thought for a few minutes. *How am I going to fix this?* Then he suddenly said, "You gotta call Milano and tell him if those kids come asking, the man they are looking for is dead as a doorbell. You hear?"

"You serious, Bus? You want me to have him kill the guy?"

"No, Fish. Have him *say* the guy is dead. Do *not* have him kill the guy. Have him *tell* those kids, he found him and he's dead. You got me?" Buster leaned closer to his old friend and raised his voice. "You got me?" he repeated louder.

"Okay, man, shit." Fish took the last drink from his beer can and handed it to Buster. "You sure you don't wanna make some money? We really need a counterfeit guy."

"Fish, tell Milano to say the guy is swimmin' with your friends at the bottom of the Pacific."

"Okay, okay," Fish said, smacking Buster in the abs with the back of his open hand. "It was good to see you, buddy. Call me if you change your mind about the job," he said and walked out the door.

Buster watched as his old friend hopped onto his motorcycle and drove off into the dark.

CHAPTER 13

The relationship between the dreamers
and the stars
is symbiotic.
You look up;
they look down—
flashing and smiling,
grinning and piling
behind the doors of the night
guarded by the moon,
that bull-faced bruiser of a bouncer
and the protector
of our exclusive nightclub curtains,
as if to say
you are the stars.
And there are certain cases
in which you are
because
besides your dreams,
there is only one other thing
that lasts
forever:
love.
That is because

inside these two things
time does not exist—
and if you hold hands
with someone
while you sleep,
your dreams often kiss.

"**M**orning," Alison heard Linda call as she walked through the front door of her house.

"Quiet," Jean told her. "Alison is asleep."

"With James?"

"Yes."

Alison lifted her head and looked at James, who had fallen asleep not more than twenty minutes after he came over. His head rested on the arm of the couch. His face was a shadow of coarse blond hairs. He had the king of hearts stuck to his temple.

"She's still the only one who can get James to turn his brain off and fall asleep in a thunderstorm, you know."

"I know, Joe," Jean said.

Alison could hear her mother washing dishes as she talked to Linda.

"Remember when your boys were little and they would sleep over here?"

"I remember *why*," Linda said.

Alison remembered why as well. Linda's house was rarely safe enough for them to sleep in.

"Alison used to tell him her little stories to get him to fall back asleep, remember?"

"I do."

****

When James and Luke were young, they spent many nights at Sarah and Alison's house. Sometimes David would go get them and bring them over. Sometimes they would just come over without being asked. This was before James grew strong enough to push his father back the way that he had been pushed his whole life. This was before holding hands meant more than just holding hands. James would hold Alison's hand in his, bridging the gap between their sleeping bags on the front porch. Alison would tell him stories—long, ridiculous stories about thieves and magicians, stars and oceans. Anything she could think of that she could make beautiful, she told him. She put them together and stitched in a plot and a twist. He lay there holding her hand, wondering if there really were things out there, things he had never seen that were as beautiful as she made them sound.

As James and Luke grew older, they stopped coming over to get away from their dad. They stayed home instead to protect their mom. They stopped spending the night at Sarah and Alison's house almost completely, except for during thunderstorms. It was when it rained hardest that James could not sleep. He would lie in bed and count everything in his room from ceiling tiles to things that were round to things that were square to things that started with each letter of the alphabet to things that were smaller than an apple. He counted all the way into the morning.

The first story Alison ever told James during a thunderstorm was about a cowboy who wrestled alligators and ate them. By the time she could figure out how she wanted to end it, James was snoring next to her. It had been almost twenty years since the alligator story, and Alison was pretty sure the thunder still kept him from closing his eyes at night because he'd asked to come over every thunderstorm since.

She was not surprised this time when James called at four in the morning—even though they had just left each other less than four hours ago. After only three strikes of lightning, the power was out. She knew it was him before she even answered the phone on the second ring. "You suck," she said when she did.

"You have 496 eyelashes."

"Thanks. You too," she replied and added a yawn.

"Can I come over and help you organize the refrigerator?"

"No."

"Hang Christmas lights?"

"It's July."

"Tell me a story."

"No."

"Watch TV."

"Fine." She could feel him smiling through the phone. She hung up, grabbed her pillow, and waited for him on the couch. He sat down so she could put the pillow on his lap and lay her head on it. She closed her eyes as he began shuffling a deck of cards and playing what she imagined was solitaire.

"You suck," she said again, not opening her eyes. "But I think I love you."

James stopped playing his game and kissed her forehead. "That's good because I've loved you ever since the day I met you."

She smiled without opening her eyes. James returned to his game while she listened to the weatherman on television. James was the only guy she ever felt comfortable sleeping with, possibly because they had never had sex. Also, she had never said, "I love you," to any man but her father.

****

Henry sat in a chair at the police station, waiting to talk with Officer Bob. Bob walked over to Henry and shook his hand. They made small talk for a few minutes like they always did until Bob said, "Let's go into the office."

When they got to the office and the door had been closed, Henry handed Bob a traveler's check. "This should cover it," Henry said.

"How long we gonna keep doing this?" Bob asked Henry.

"As long as he wants us to."

Bob put the check in an envelope in his desk drawer and scratched his hairless chin. "<i>He</i> meaning God or <i>he</i> meaning David?"

"Both," Henry said, patting Bob on his left shoulder with one hand and leaning on his walker with his other hand.

"I just wish this would have never happened," Bob said, unlocking his office door for the pastor.

"Everything happens for a reason, friend," Henry said, opening the door. "Everything," he said again with one half of a smile and pushed his walker out the door.

The next Monday, Bob and Josie would use the money from the traveler's check to pay for the scratch tickets that Alison and Sarah won with—the fake scratch tickets that Buster made for them to win with. And when they won, it would be their own father's money they would

- 163 -

be taking, not the gas station's or the state's. Henry told Bob, "It was a deal between an officer of the law, an officer of God, and a regular man just trying to take care of his family."

****

Bob sat at his desk and remembered the phone call he had made to Henry. It was so long ago when he called and asked the old pastor for guidance.

"I think most cops need guidance," Henry agreed. Then he laughed to let Bob know he was only joking.

But Bob did not return the amusement. It had been almost a week after Charles's car accident.

"You know that car accident with your neighbor up there on Fifty-Nine?"

"Uh-huh."

"Well, his death wasn't an accident."

"What on earth are you talking about, Bob?"

"Charles Bradley Bluff was shot. That accident didn't kill him."

"Whose gun was it?"

"It was Charles's."

"So he shot himself?"

"Not quite. There was another set of prints on that gun, Pastor."

"Whose prints for God's sake, Bob? Just tell me what you are trying to tell me!"

"David Robbins killed Charles Bradley Bluff."

It took hours of contemplation and prayer before Henry came up with his decision and an agreement was made. Henry told David to leave town. He told him that there were people who would understand and there were people who wouldn't. But it wasn't up to them. It was up to God. "The law is the law," he said. "And it's better for everyone to just think that it was an accident. It would be better for your wife and your kids. It would be better for Charles's wife and kids too."

David shook his head and then Henry's hand. Henry promised to watch after David's wife and children.

"I will send money, as soon as I get some. Can you give it to my kids without them knowing it's me or what I did?"

"I will take on that responsibility," Henry said, giving David a hug wrapped up in the Holy Spirit. "We will bear this cross together. And the Lord will forgive us both one day."

CHAPTER 14

God is either unavailable
or on the other line.
Press 1
for forgiveness.
Press 2 for guidance.
Press 3 for hope.
If you are suffering,
stay on the line
for his only son.
If this is an emergency,
hang up and dial 911.

B ecause of the rain, the restaurant was empty that morning. Doug had just left for the day. So Sarah, James, Alison, Luke, and Trisha were all sitting in a booth with one another in silence. Sarah was rereading a Tom Robbins book. Luke was totaling his score to an "Are You a Pushover" quiz in *Cosmo*. Alison was reading *Automotive World* and writing her poetry in the margins. James was checking the statistics in his brain against those printed in a *Sports Illustrated*. And Trisha was reading a church bulletin. Every two minutes, she leaned over to James and asked him what a word meant. "What is *greev-ee-ance*?" she asked, scooting her pamphlet toward James and pointing in the middle of the page.

"It's gree-vance," he explained. "It means injustice," he added, not looking up from his magazine.

Sarah accidentally let out a quick laugh.

"Hey, it's not funny when people don't know things," Trisha said, tapping the back of Sarah's book with a pudgy digit. Sarah kept reading. Trisha tapped the cover of her book again. "I am talking to you."

"Oh, I'm sorry. I just read something really funny," Sarah tried.

"Oh," she said. "I thought you were laughing at me. I'm sorry too … for jumping on conclusions."

James bit the side of his cheek.

But Sarah laughed loudly. "This book is so funny," she said quickly.

"I guess. Maybe I should borrow it," Trisha said.

Luke sighed. "You guys made me mess up my score."

James glanced over the top of Luke's magazine. "Thirty-six. You are a doormat."

"Thanks. Hey! Oh, man," he whined, looking down at the explanation of the scores. "I *am* a doormat!"

"I want to do it. Let me see," Alison said, snatching the *Cosmo* from Luke.

"What am I supposed to read then?" Luke asked.

"You can share with me," Trisha said, coughing without covering her mouth and then sliding the church bulletin closer to Luke so that he could read it at the same time as she did.

"No, thanks, I'll look at cars with Alison," Luke told her. But he grew bored after only a few minutes and got up to change the channel on the TV behind the bar to *Oprah*. He sat intently while his friends continued reading. He watched an entire show, which was about makeovers with an admiration that none of his friends would ever quite fully understand.

****

When Luke first moved to Jasper County, he had very often thought of himself as an alien because he was so different from every other kid he had ever met. He was half the size of other children his age and three shades darker. His hair resembled a freshly cleaned chalkboard eraser instead of a Barbie doll's hair, which was smooth and straight like the hair of all the other kids he knew. Even the black Barbie doll didn't have hair like his. He couldn't figure it out. And no one he knew had skin as dark as his. He watched *Oprah* with his new family, who looked nothing like him. He liked Oprah because she was always happy. He liked people who were happy. She laughed when she talked with her guests. And when you are a child, people who laugh are the most beautiful people in the world. He liked her because she looked like him. Sometimes he thought maybe, just maybe, she was his real mother. He wanted to go on the show and have her help him figure out how to get bigger and grow muscles. He wanted her to teach him how not to want to play with dolls. She helped a lot of people. And *if* she was his real mother, she would help him.

As he got older, he had *almost* completely gotten over the idea of Oprah being his real mother. But he still adored her, talked about her the way Trisha and Buster talked about Jesus, saying things like "I'd have done it, too, but if Oprah ever found out …" It was something about Luke that his friends just got used to like the cowboy boots and that gaudy belt buckle.

****

When Sarah asked her first table how they were doing, they told her, "Water and an iced tea."

"That's good to hear," she said, unsurprised by the lack of common courtesy. She surveyed their faces to see if her response elicited an irked apology. She was granted the irked but not the apology. She said nothing and walked away. Then she called, "I'll be right back with those," over her shoulder.

Sarah couldn't stay any longer because the lady who ordered the water had plopped her right boob in her pudgy toddler's mouth without so much as a blanket, sweater, or paper napkin to conceal this emotional but necessary feeding frenzy between a mother and her son. There were white bubbles forming around the ring of her nipple that went slip-sliding down the child's chin. What Sarah would have liked to ask is if the lady would have liked to order a glass of milk as well, so that she could put her boob away and her coworker would be able to drink her iced tea without getting either turned on or puking all over the menu. *How busy can a person possibly be that she is forced to multitask, having a business meeting, eating lunch, and breastfeeding her toddler in a smoke-filled bar?* Sarah wondered. Alison had told her once that feeding a baby was like smoking cigarettes, which meant that, in Alison's opinion, it should be allowed anywhere and anytime. Sarah told her that there should be an age limit, "like two or three, tops." But again Alison disagreed. "Nah, you can't regulate the way that mothers nurture their children." Sarah finally gave up on the argument but told Alison that "anywhere, anytime, and any age" meant that there might be quite a few coughing kids wanting to have a conversation with her about why she was letting their mothers feed them next to a beer tap and an ashtray as a result of such a revolutionary philosophy. Alison just smiled and said, "I am a fucking philosopher, aren't I?"

****

When Trisha and Buster went to watch the videotape they had asked Alison to make of their wedding, Trisha was so embarrassed by the vulgarity in Alison's commentary that she ended up taking back a stainless-steel knife set to get the money to have it professionally edited. Alison apologized over and over again, saying she had had too much champagne and keg beer and that *it really was* "the most beautiful fucking ceremony" she had ever seen.

Trisha should have known. But no matter how long any of them had known Alison, her incessant use of the f-word still took them by surprise at times. The truth was that Alison developed her dirty mouth from the mornings she spent with her dad in the garage before he went to work. At one point or another, it became an early morning ritual for the both of them to work on the car together. And Sarah had never really heard her dad cuss. But Alison told her that that car made him cuss the way mosquitoes made you itch.

The only time during the day that David wasn't at work was when he was trying to get the car to run so that he could go to work. Alison saw her opportunity to spend time with him and embraced it. She would wait outside early in the morning for her dad to come out and start the car. She would dribble the basketball or ride her bike up and down the driveway or play catch with their dog. When David came out with his coffee, he would say, "You're up early."

"Uh-huh," she'd say. Then she'd ask, "Think it'll start?"

"We'll see."

That was how their conversation always started. The car, on the other hand, rarely started. And as the months passed, David was no longer angry when it didn't. *Calamity has a funny way of bringing people together.* He explained what was wrong and what the possible problems could be and what the parts were and what they did. Alison learned quickly. And she had never had a problem with getting dirty. They both crawled underneath the car with their flashlights, examining the leaks that were okay and the leaks that weren't okay. So it was his crappy Oldsmobile that brought Alison and her dad closer than fathers and daughters usually became. Because either he taught her what she always wanted to know or maybe it was that she always wanted to know whatever it was he taught her. Either way, when her dad left, in their family's only car, Alison was slapped on both cheeks. That car, not her dad, was the only thing Alison ever really knew on the inside. But she was not prepared for either one to run out.

Jackpot

CHAPTER 15

Truth is a tricky thing,
always changing,
rearranging
himself
in the most inappropriate
place
at the most inappropriate
time;
you show me yours,
and I'll show you mine.
But truth be told,
and you may have to tell him twice,
the truth would be so damn
nice.
Whether it's your
truth or her truth
or his,
its intentions
are usually good,
and it almost always stays
when it should.

David and Officer Bob stood there in the cemetery for a few minutes, not knowing what to do or say. "It's kind of like being at my own funeral. I mean, I know it's not *my* headstone. But I am a dead guy standing in front of a headstone," David said finally.

"Well, now that you're dead, you know you can't come back here anymore. I mean it this time. Not even if you stay out of sight. We would both go to jail if it comes out what you did and how me and Henry knew about it. Now we need to go. We gotta do this thing quick while your family is at work."

"Just give me a minute," he said.

Bob waved to the headstone but said nothing. He left David and went to wait in his car.

David stood alone in the shining sun, looking at Charles's name carved into that stone. "I wanted to tell you that I am not coming back and I forgive you and I forgive myself. You just got drowned in all that liquor, didn't you?" he asked the gravestone. There were tears coming up to his eyes, and his voice cracked in half when he said, "I remember you when you were kind. It was a long time ago, Charles, but I remember when James was born, you were so happy. You couldn't stop grinning or kissing that baby. You covered that kid all up in slobber every time you held him." He laughed away another series of tears that were pressing on his eyes. "It's the liquor that's mean, not the man. I hope God let you up there, and I hope he lets me up there too," he said. Then he turned and walked to the car he had bought for his family and got in.

Bob followed David in his cruiser to Jean's house. David parked the car in his old driveway. Bob parked in the street. David sat for several minutes, looking at all the flowers his wife had planted after he left. When he got out of the car, the dog came limping toward him, full speed. David bent down and put his face next to Bob's. The two of them stayed like that, David on one knee and Bob sitting still except his tail as they faced one another until Officer Bob called, "Okay, David, we have got to get out of here." His voice was more sympathetic than demanding. David got up and got into Officer Bob's car, leaving the one he had just bought in his old driveway with the keys inside.

Bob and David didn't talk on the three-hour drive back to David's house. David just read the paper, worked on the crossword, and looked out the window while Bob silently stared straight ahead. When Bob pulled up to David's apartment, he heaved a sigh filled with sorrow. "That was a nice thing you did, getting that car for your family. I'll tell them we got it out of the police impound lot," Bob said.

"There isn't a police impound lot anywhere near Jasper County!" David laughed.

"I'll tell them Buster stole it then."

David laughed even harder. He shook his head back and forth.

"No, don't do that," he said. Then he waited for Bob to say something else so he didn't have to get out of the car. Once he got out, he knew he would never see Bob or anyone in Jasper County again.

Bob was silent.

"Thank you. Thank you for everything," David said.

Bob nodded.

"They named that dog after you, ya know?" David told Bob.

He smiled at David.

****

Bob wanted to tell David that Jean had named that dog after him too. But he didn't. Instead, he called, "You forgot your newspaper," to David as he walked away.

"Keep it." David looked over his shoulder to answer. "Dead guys don't need to read the news."

****

When Bob called Jean up at work to let her know he had found a car for free in the impound lot and put it in the driveway for her family, she was ecstatic. He could hear her clapping her hands together over and over again. She dropped the phone and picked it back up.

"Bob, you ... How ... how did you do that?" she stammered. "You are just the best police officer in the world. You are so kind. How can we repay you? You should take some money. How much should I give you?"

It broke Bob's heart to take all the credit that David deserved.

"No, Jean. I told you, it was free. I don't need any money."

"But you found it. You should take it."

"Our car is just fine," he insisted.

"Well, bless your heart," she said. "God bless your kind heart."

****

Jean hung up the phone and explained what Bob had told her to Linda, Gloria, and Boo Boo. The four women held hands and jumped up and down in a circle so many times Boo Boo's wig came loose. She let go of Linda's hand to hold it down as she continued to jump.

****

"Who's at your house?" James asked, eyeing the shiny gray Ford sitting in the driveway.

"I have no idea," Alison said.

"Maybe Oprah bought us all cars," Trisha said excitedly and looked toward her empty driveway. "Nope," she said sadly, "I didn't get one."

"I think you have to be on the show to get one," Luke told her.

"We got a new car!" Jean yelled, sprinting out the door, down the porch steps, and toward them. "We got a new car! We got a new car!"

"When, and how the fuck did we get a new car?" Alison asked.

"Today!" Jean exclaimed. "Bob got it for free from the police impound! Look! Isn't it pretty?"

Alison could tell the car had been there for a while because the excitement pouring out of her mom seemed to have been fermenting inside her for at least a few hours. Jean held up the keys. "Who's going to take it for a test drive?"

Alison grabbed the keys and went running toward the car. Jean, James, Luke, Trisha, and Sarah all smashed themselves in, and Alison drove them around the neighborhood. They were all talking a mile a minute. It was probably uncomfortable being smashed up against one another in the backseat. But being behind the wheel was exhilarating.

Alison knew she was beaming. She shouted at everything they passed. "Hey, squirrel!" she yelled out the window. "Look how fast I'm going!"

Everyone laughed.

"Hey, post office, check out my turn signal!"

They laughed almost the whole time. Alison couldn't keep her mouth shut, and it cracked them all up. "Say something to the stoplight!" Trisha shouted from under the weight of Sarah's body.

"Hey, stoplight, you wanna hear my new horn?" Alison screamed. Then she laid on the horn several times in the melody of "Jingle Bells." When they got back to the driveway, Alison's voice was hoarse and her stomach hurt from laughing. She was laughing so hard she thought she might pee her pants. She ran inside to use the bathroom and noticed the light on the answering machine blinking. She crossed her legs together, held her crotch with her hands, and then hit play. "This is Anthony Milano. I have news about David Robbins. Please call me back as soon as you get this message. 306-843-9991." Beep. Alison stared at the machine. She hit play again. "This is Anthony Milano. I have news about David Robbins. Please call me back as soon as you get this message. 306-843-9991." Beep. She played it again. And again. Until Sarah walked in.

"Alison?" Sarah asked, her voice wavering as their eyes met. She looked at Alison's wet jeans. "Did you pee your pants?"

Alison looked down at her legs. She hadn't even realized she had done it.

"What's wrong?" Sarah asked, looking at Alison's face and then the light on the answering machine. Alison hit play. Sarah touched Alison's shoulder. "Go change," she said after hearing the message. "And we will call him."

Alison didn't move.

"Ali?"

"What do you think he found out?" Alison answered.

"I don't know, Alison. Go change and we will call him. I promise. As soon as you change."

Alison began walking slowly to her bedroom. The picture of her dad still lay broken on the floor. She picked it up and began to cry. "Dad,

I'm afraid to hear what he has to say," she said, bringing the picture into her chest and lying down on her bare mattress. The sheets and quilt still lay on the floor, along with everything she had knocked off of her desk yesterday. Sarah gave a soft knock on the frame of the door. But Alison didn't move.

"Whatever it is," Sarah said walking into Alison's room and lying down next to her on her bed, "we are going to be okay." Then she added, "You will be okay."

Alison looked at Sarah's face only an inch away from her own. She looked just as scared as Alison was. "I don't want to call him."

"I know," Sarah said, lifting up her shirt and wiping Alison's nose with the hem.

Alison gave a soft laugh. "That was gross."

Sarah smiled.

"Very sweet," Alison added. "But fucking gross."

"You're the one with pee pants," Sarah told Alison as she sat up.

Jean was standing in the doorway. Alison could tell by her face that her mom had played the message. "Who is Anthony Milano?" Jean asked.

Sarah sat up. Then Alison sat up and grabbed Sarah's hand, trying to urge her to explain so she didn't have to. Sarah looked at Alison and then Jean. "He is someone who was trying to help us find Dad," she said.

Jean came over to the bed and squeezed in between them.

"Okay," Jean said, squeezing Alison's right leg and Sarah's left leg. "If that's what you want to do, let's call him back."

One by one, they got up and went to the kitchen phone. Sarah picked up the phone and began to dial. She pushed the speaker button so that everyone could hear.

"Hello?"

"Hi, Anthony. This is Sarah Robbins."

"Hello, Sarah," he said and then took a long breath.

Alison looked at Sarah with tears beginning in her eyes.

"I'm afraid your father is dead."

Sarah dropped the phone. Alison's knees buckled, and she collapsed to the floor. Jean stood frozen.

"What … how?" Sarah stammered.

"Are you sure?" Alison added, her voice so quiet it was barely audible.

"About five years ago. The coroner's report said a heart attack."

"Are you sure?" Alison asked again, trying to make her voice louder.

"I'm sure. I can send you the death certificate if it will help your family move forward."

"Thank you," Jean said as she sat down on the floor next to Alison.

"I am real sorry. On a personal note, your friends kicked the shit outta my kid. He's okay, but he's learned a lesson and he's very sorry."

"What?" Jean asked.

"His son did that to Ali's face," Sarah clarified for her mother.

Jean didn't speak. She looked as if she was replaying some scene in her head.

"Feel free to call me if you ever need anything again."

"Okay," Sarah said, sitting on the tiled floor with Alison and Jean. The three of them embraced one another as the dial tone sang in the background.

"What are you guys doing in here?" Alison heard James call as the front door creaked, followed by the sound of voices and laughter that softened when he closed the door behind him. The footsteps paralleled the beating of her heart in her chest.

She looked up at him. "He's dead," she said, trying to make her voice louder than the beating of her heart.

"David?" he asked, looking from her face to Sarah's and then Jean's.

"Yes, David," Jean said, and the dog came running.

He nudged his nose into Jean's hand. She picked him up and held him. James sat cross-legged on the floor next to Alison. He put his arms around her and held on tight as she began to sob. His arms felt strong, the way her dad's used to when he held her, comforted her. The door creaked open again, and there were more footsteps and voices. The rhythm braided itself through the air. Everything began to blur—the voices, dial tone, and light strips where dust particles danced. The last thing Alison remembered was James kissing her softly on the forehead.

****

After Alison fainted, James picked her up and carried her to her room. She opened her eyes briefly and sleepily smiled at him. He laid her on her bed, picked up the sheet that was crumpled up on the floor, and gently covered her with it, tucking it around her thin frame. He picked up a pillow too, lifted her head, and carefully slid it under. Then he began to clean her room. Each time the minute hand touched the twelve, he looked at her to see if she had stirred. She looked peaceful. Forty-five minutes had passed before she finally opened her eyes and met his across the room. He came and sat next to her on the bed, gauging her expression for the condition she was in.

"Was it a dream?" she asked. "Is my dad dead?"

"It wasn't a dream," James said, leaning close to her face and sweeping a strand of hair behind her ear. She appeared to be deep in thought.

"Then he didn't leave me on purpose," she said finally.

"No one would ever leave you if they didn't have to," he said, taking her hand and lacing his fingers around hers.

Her eyes appeared to sweep the room. "Thank you for cleaning up my mess."

"Anytime."

There were several voices outside, along with music and laughter.

"There are a lot of people waiting for you to wake up. Henry wanted to know if you want to go to church."

"What time is it?" she asked.

"Four thirty."

"I'll tell you what I want," she said, sitting up in bed. "I want to change out of these pee pants and go to the store. I am going to buy bubbles."

"Bubbles?"

"Yeah, my dad used to get them for me and Sarah all the time. He would blow them for us, and we would run all over the yard chasing them. It was really fun," she said with a smile.

"Okay," he said and smiled back.

"Then I will go to church." She got up from the bed and went to her closet. She stood there for a long time, examining the contents. She finally selected a dress, put it over her arm, and took it into the bathroom with her.

James went outside where Henry, Trisha, Buster, their kids, Sarah, Jean, Linda, Boo Boo, Gloria, Bob, Josie, the Joes, even Doug, and the Grangers too were talking to one another on the porch. They all looked at him as he stepped outside.

"She wants to go to the store and buy bubbles," he explained. "Then she will go to church."

Sarah looked at him approvingly. "That actually sounds like a pretty good idea."

"Remember how all the kids used to run around outside, chasing bubbles all over the place?" Linda said to Jean and smiled.

"I do," she said, grabbing ahold of her shoulder and laughing. "Trisha always tried to eat them." She looked over at Trisha. "Remember that, honey? You thought they would turn into bubblegum in your mouth."

"Yeah," Trisha said, chuckling. "Of course, they don't though," she added, but it sounded more like a question than a statement.

Buster wrapped his arms around her from behind and pulled her close to him. "Girl, you'd eat a branch right off a tree," he said.

The front door opened, and Alison walked out, looking the prettiest James had ever seen her. She was wearing light makeup and had combed her hair so that it was smooth and shiny. Her lips were a soft pink, like inside of a grapefruit. And her green eyes sparkled under the thin fan of her darkened eyelashes. A flowery dress danced around her frame, and the breeze blew the soft fabric. Terrence ran up to her holding an armful of bubble bottles.

"Me and Jennifer had these. You can have them," he said, looking up at her.

"Thank you. You want me to blow those around the yard for you after church?" she said, smiling down at him.

Gina D'Agosta

"Yes! Yes! Pwease," he told her, dropping all the bottles at her feet. "You look pretty," he added, giving her a hug.

"Thank you," she said, hugging him back. "I guess I'm ready for church then," she announced when she let go. She bent over, grabbed a bottle of bubbles, and put it in her purse. "One for the road," she explained. Then she walked down the steps and took James's hand, and they walked to church, followed by the large percentage of the town's population now gathered in the yard.

****

Henry softly grunted as he got up from the chair that he was sitting in. He leaned on his walker for support. When he was fully upright—or as upright as his body got these days—he pushed the walker, walked, pushed, and walked until he was at the podium. He tapped on the microphone and said, "Don't anybody fall asleep out there. This one is important." The congregation laughed. "I'm serious," he said. Then he laughed. He paused, and the church was quiet except for the buzz of fans and insects and the soft sobs of the people who had gathered to celebrate David Robbins. "I am, by now, an old man. I lose friends every other day it seems." He looked around the church. David's family and friends were all mixed in with his family and friends. Every face he saw as he looked around was a face he cared about. "If you haven't heard by now, we were informed of David Robbins's death today. For me, he is not gone and never will be. I see his face in his children. I see his heart in his friends, his neighbors. He gave all of us something. Many of us are bound together by him, because of him. We are all better people for having known him." Henry saw people begin to cry. One. By. One. Like dominos. "David once asked me a powerful question. He said, 'What do you do when you've already done everything you can?' I thought for a minute. Then I told him, 'Something you never thought you could.' David was worried about his family. He had regrets, mistakes. All of us do. But it plagued him. He didn't think he was a good enough dad or husband. But he was good. He was a good man. We all make mistakes, I told him. We learn and we grow. I guess what I'm saying is you have

- 182 -

to let your worries go, float up to God. Enjoy what you have. Because what you don't have, you don't need." Henry paused and looked at Bob and Josie. "Some sins are mistakes. But not all mistakes are sins." Then he looked at Buster. "Sometimes, friends, mistakes are just mistakes." He sighed and looked down at his wedding band. "Do you know why I became a pastor?" he said, looking back up, this time with glossy eyes, "because when Pam agreed to marry me, I thought God had performed a miracle."

Everyone laughed. Some of the older people nodded their heads up and down. Pam looked at her husband and smiled through tears.

"And when I saw her walk down that aisle, I knew I owed him big. I mean *big*. But the thing of it is … I was always meant to become a pastor. Just like I was always meant to marry that beautiful woman in the front row pulling tissue out of her dress." Many people turned in their pews to look at Pam. Pam looked up just as she was about to blow her nose. "I'm sorry, Pam," Henry apologized to his wife for bringing so much attention to her. Then he continued, "David's wife and children learned something about their father today. He didn't leave them." He paused and looked at Jean, Sarah, and Alison. Then he repeated what he had just said, "He did not leave you." James took ahold of Alison's hand. She took ahold of Sarah's. Sarah took Jean's, and she took Linda's. Henry watched as each person in each row took each other's hand. "God told him it was time to go. He would never have left if God hadn't've asked. God's got a plan for all of us. Your sins and your mistakes are in there. His forgiveness is a part of that plan. And your forgiveness of others is also a part of that plan. Forgive David for leaving us because it wasn't his plan. It was God's, and you can't stay mad at God 'cause he gave you David in the first place. He also gave us football Sunday."

****

When the Mass was over, Jean took out a compact to check her makeup and shared it with Boo Boo, who gasped when she saw her reflection. Boo Boo's makeup was running and evidence of someone else underneath was beginning to show, like a child dressed as a clown surfacing from bobbing for apples at a Halloween party only to realize that she had lost both the game and half of her identity.

"Why didn't you tell me my makeup was coming off?" Boo Boo turned and asked Gloria.

"Lo siento. I didn't ree-lize," Gloria apologized. "You always look nice."

Jean smoothed her own makeup and wiped her eyes; then she looked at Boo Boo. She hadn't even noticed.

"There's nothing wrong with who you are under there," Jean said, surprising herself.

"You are one hundred percent right. Thanks for reminding me."

****

Alison walked back behind the altar. "Henry," she said, knocking on the wall beside the altar.

He was in the middle of putting the wine away. He set it down on the counter beside the wall and looked up at her.

"Yes, Alison?"

"You can tell God it's okay. That I forgive him."

"He knows."

****

After church, Jean, Linda, the Joes, Pam, Henry, Gloria, Boo Boo, Sarah, Luke, Alison, James, Buster, Trisha, Terrence, Jennifer, Doug, Bob, and Josie walked back to Jean's house. Henry and Pam walked slowly behind at a snail's pace leaving tiny walker-wheel trails through the leftover puddles on the sidewalk. Pam had slowed down her entire life for Henry and always seemed grateful about it. Alison kept glancing back over her shoulder to watch the way Pam's steps mirrored her husband's next to his walker. Alison blew bubbles as she walked. Terrence, Jennifer, and Trisha ran ahead to catch them. Luke suddenly ran in front of them all. "Simon says do this, 'Cha-cha-cha-cha-cha-cha!'" He skipped from side to side.

Terrence and Jennifer said, "Cha-cha-cha-cha-cha-cha," and skipped from side to side.

"Simon says do this," he called over his shoulder at the giggling children. "Ooo, ow, ow, oo, la, la." He threw his hands up in the air and back and forth. Terrence and Jennifer laughed and did the same.

"Do this." Luke shook his hips from side to side.

"Simon didn't say!" Terrence and Jennifer screamed.

"Come on! Shake those hips," Luke said, shaking his hips as he walked.

"Nooooo!" Terrence yelled.

"You." Luke pointed to Trisha. "Shake those hips."

"Simon's got to say," Trisha said, putting her face against Buster's arm and giggling into his tattoos.

"I don't know who this Simon cat is, but my baby girl only shakes her hips for me. So he better not ask," Buster said, holding his wife close as they walked.

"Okay, okay," Luke said. Then he yelled, "Simon says, 'Shake those hips!'"

Trisha broke free of Buster, turned around, and wiggled her large round butt at Luke.

"That's the straw, and I'm a camel with a busted back," Buster yelled, running after Luke.

Luke let out a high-pitched scream and ran toward Jean's house. Buster chased him, letting up when he got too close. They zigzagged across the front lawn. Luke ducked behind the side of the house and emerged with the garden hose.

"Oh man, you don't want to do that," Buster said, looking at Luke and shaking his head from side to side.

Luke smiled. "Simon said I had to," Luke told Buster and lifted the hose.

"Tell Simon you ain't doin' it!"

"Well, maybe you should shake them hips too then, Buster."

"What? Oh, man, you gotta be kidding."

"Simon says, 'Shake those hips … and say, 'Ah cha cha cha!'"

Buster pressed his lips together and flexed his biceps. He turned around for the rest of the group to see. "You really think he can make me shake my can by pointing that hose at my balls?"

Trisha looked like she was just about to scold Buster for saying "balls" when Luke bent down and turned the nozzle on the hose, pointed it at Buster, and soaked his entire backside. Luke dropped the hose and ran inside, the whole time screaming like a girl. Buster wrung out his ponytail, and like a dog, he shook his right and then his left leg. All the group, especially Terrence and Jennifer, were on the sidewalk laughing.

It was just after Buster wrung out his ponytail that Alison saw Sarah pull a worn-out piece of paper from her wallet. It was permanently creased from being folded and refolded. Alison knew on that paper were the names of every single person she vowed revenge against, handwritten in different colors on different days—people who had complained, not tipped, made her work too hard, almost got her fired, treated her like a child, harassed and disrespected her. She watched her sister look at the paper for a long time and then wad it up into a paper ball and throw it into the street. Alison walked up the driveway to where their new car sat. She ran her hands along it as she walked past. She reached into her purse and touched the tape cassette no one had noticed her pull out of the car cassette player when she first got in. It was Bruce Springsteen's *The River*. Her dad's favorite. She kept her hand on the cassette in her purse as she walked up the porch steps where everyone had gathered.

"You know who I feel sorry for?" Trisha was saying to Bob.

"Who's that?" he asked, finally putting down a newspaper he had been holding since church.

"Porcupines," Trisha answered confidently.

"What?" Luke said. "Why?" He looked from Jean's face to Trisha's to Linda's.

Linda shrugged. Henry and Pam looked just as confused.

"Because they can't hug one another," Trisha said, throwing her arms around Jean.

"Aww, baby, that is so nice," Buster said, rubbing Trisha's back.

Jean picked up Bob's paper. "If you are all done, can I have it? I like to do the crosswords."

"It's yours," he told her.

"Hey!" she exclaimed after she opened it up. "You only have one left. It's easy. Someone hand me a pen." Alison handed her mother a pen from her purse. "To let go," she said out loud. "It's seven letters. F-o-r-g-i-v-e," she said, writing it into the crossword. "First time I've ever finished one."

Jennifer was sitting on the ground next to Henry's leg. She was meowing and licking her hands as if they were paws. Luke looked down at Jennifer. Then he looked over at Buster.

"Hey, Buster, did you ever think Jennifer wants to be a cat so bad because you are always referring to everyone as cats?"

Buster looked at Luke and seemed deep in thought for a minute.

"No," he said, shaking his head from side to side. "I had never even thought of that! You oughta say what you think more often!"

"You are so smart," Trisha said, throwing her arms around Luke.

"This cat—" Buster stopped and put his hand over his mouth. He took his hand down and continued, "I mean, dude ... this dude is a genius." He pointed toward Luke with one of his thumbs.

"Come here, Bob." Jean snapped her fingers and called the dog up onto the porch.

Alison grabbed Sarah's hand and squeezed. "Did she just fucking call the dog ... *Bob*?" she whispered, her eyes wide.

"Yeah," Sarah said slowly. "I think she did."

The dog did a three-legged sprint toward Jean. Then he hopped onto her lap and dropped a soggy balled-up piece of paper between her legs.

"What's this, honey? Did you eat someone's homework?"

Alison didn't have to guess at what it was. She knew it was Sarah's list. She laughed, not because it was better than crying, not because she knew her dad wasn't coming back, but because her heart finally felt full. She thought about what Henry said at the church: *Enjoy what you have 'cause what you don't have, you don't need.* She looked around the porch at all the people she loved and watched them talking and laughing. James leaned over, put his arms on the sides of her face, and softly kissed her. *So this is the plan Henry was talking about,* she thought as she kissed him back.

AUTHOR'S NOTE: A WORD ON BOO BOO

I chose to use the word transvestite to describe the character Boo Boo because this story takes place in the 90s when this was a popular word used to describe a man who dresses as a woman. It is important to note that today many people consider this term offensive. This word does not fully encompass Boo Boo's unique bi-gender personhood. No matter how small Boo Boo's role is in the this story, he deserves our respect whether he is dressed as a man and acting as a man or she is dressed as a woman and acting as a woman. Labels can be problematic. Boo Boo would tell you that the best practice is to ask what a person prefers to be called rather than using a blanket categorization. For Boo Boo, it is simple. As a man, he prefers to be called Boo Boo. As a woman, she prefers to be called Boo Boo. Although Boo Boo is comfortable talking about both gender identities, he chooses to keep these personas separate. Consequently, no one has ever met them both. Perhaps someday, someone special will.

On a side note, Boo Boo has always used the bathroom according to his very real gender identity at the time and never given two shits what anyone has to say about it.

ABOUT THE AUTHOR

Gina D'Agosta graduated from the University of Nebraska with Bachelors Degrees in Arts and Sciences in English and Sociology. *Sinners, Saints, and Scratch Tickets* is her debut novel. She resides in Arlington Heights, Il with her husband and two children where she is at work on her second novel.

www.ingramcontent.com/pod-product-compliance
Lightning Source LLC
Chambersburg PA
CBHW050533260626

47157CB00004B/1583